Men Of Discretion

MEN OF
DISCRETION

KEVIN MUNIZ

ISBN: 979-8-89860-858-3

CONTENTS

PREFACE

Since the dawn of the universe, an overarching authority has governed humanity. In certain instances, the identity of this governing power is well-defined, while in other cases, the general populace remains unaware of those who exercise control. Civilizations worldwide have operated under governing bodies that establish the rules necessary for societal function. The fundamental aim of these structures is to foster a stable society that thrives in a healthy environment. Nonetheless, this process may not always succeed in its intended outcomes. Control is an aspiration shared by many, as it confers both freedom and authority.

One of the advantages of occupying a position of

significant power is the inherent ability to evade account-ability more easily than ordinary citizens. However, the delegation of authority to individuals ill-suited for such roles can have perilous consequences. When this misallocation occurs, the rule of law and higher institutions can become ineffective and lose their intended function. This disruption may compel otherwise law-abiding citizens to engage in unethical behavior, resulting in societal chaos characterized by intense and polarizing disagreements. Ultimately, this breakdown can precipitate the decline of social order.

This book is, by no means, an attempt to change your mind on how the world should be ruled. It is a unique way to give you a perspective of, the huge responsibility of someone who holds a lot of power. In some cases, the most minute disagreements, can cause devastating consequences. What civilizations most value above all is the way in which they live. An individual's way of life not only affects how they behave, but also what the future of their country would be like. The past and the present have been critical to molding a better future for the younger generation of humans. It does not matter if someone has had power all their life, or if they have recently obtained power. The difficulty of making the right decisions day after day can drive a person who is not ready straight to insanity. Choosing the correct people to have around you is almost as important as making the smartest decisions.

One of the main factors that can cause a society to

crumble is the ambition to take more than it needs. For many years, conflict has always been about who rules what. Societies clash and war begins, and with war not only comes the destruction of people but also that of societies. The traumatic experiences of war have caused, us to learn from our previous mistakes.

Even though, trial and error are essential. It is imperative that we conduct an analysis to determine the root cause of the error. Great governmental bodies often fail to comprehend where things are going wrong. Different problems start to add up, causing complete destruction. It becomes challenging to find solutions to complicated issues. However, this does not mean we have to give up on our goal, it simply means we have to fight for what we initially believed was right.

Time has proven that there is no right formula to prevent the impulsive decisions a flawed human makes. However, when a group of highly intelligent people managed to somehow break the corrupt system filled with flaws, they found a solution. After years of perfecting and building it, they came up with something that may eventually work. The men rose to a power that was much deeper than the ones the authorities had. They understood that, to remain in control, they had to live an occult life.

The discretion of a man makes him slow to anger, and his glory is to overlook a transgression.

- PROVERB 19: 11

CHAPTER 1

THE RECRUIT

The world encompasses a complex interplay of positive and negative phenomena. One aspect that continues to elude my understanding is the array of unusual events that occur daily. In an era where information is readily accessible, the reasons behind many of these occurrences remain perplexing. Gaining a comprehensive understanding of such events presents a near-impossible challenge, as it would require one to possess a presence in multiple contexts simultaneously. Nevertheless, amidst the myriad questions that occupy my thoughts, I have managed to cultivate a sense of peace in the midst of an ever-unfolding tempest.

My life has not been impervious to these complexities.

15

Although there is no reason for me to express dissatisfaction regarding the events that have taken place thus far, a pivotal moment transpired on a mundane Tuesday night when I was only thirteen years old. It was during this time that my father, a significant figure in my life, illuminated a bright flashlight while I was still asleep. At that moment, although I was uncertain of the hour, my instincts informed me that it was not yet time to prepare for school.

"Get up, son, we are going on a trip." At that point, I was half awake and confused as to why my father was informing me that we were going on a trip. Just like most parents, they believe that education is the most important part of the development of a young person. Therefore, they ensured that I attended school every day. Nevertheless, I changed into more casual clothes and headed down the stairs, where my dad was waiting for me.

"What about Mom? Will she come with us?"

"No, just us," my dad replied while heading out of the house.

Before dawn, the neighborhood looked like a ghost town. It was early autumn; the trees were changing colors between oranges, reds, and dry brown. It was a heavenly view; the leaves fell, covering the entire terrain, and the temperature began to change to a much cooler climate in the small town of Richmond Hill.

The town was approximately an hour up north from the gorgeous city of Toronto. My father turned on his all-black compact car before heading out of the house. He would drive all the way to the national highway system, which was fairly empty, although there were a lot of freight trucks.

We continued on our peculiar journey toward an unknown destination. The realization that I was unfamiliar with the road, as well as the part of Canada we were traversing, left me with a profound sense of disorientation. After an extended period of driving, my father decided to pull over to the side of the road. While his decision to stop was not unexpected, I was intrigued by the fact that he chose to do so in a section of the highway with only two lanes—one heading north and the other south. Surrounding us were some of the most striking pine trees I had ever encountered, their beauty capturing my attention despite the uncertainty of our journey.

"What's wrong, Dad?" I asked, wanting to get a better grip on the situation.

"Somebody has been following us."

Being young and gullible, I did not understand what was truly going on.

My father opened and closed all four windows of the car. At that time, it seemed confusing to me. It was not until later in life that I found out that he was changing the windows into a stronger, bulletproof glass, and the windows would become very dark. Blocking the view of the interior. No matter how close a person stood to take a peek, even if you had the vision of a hawk. The reason he did not have them permanently removed was that the glass was so heavy that it could damage the car.

"Wait here," my father said.

Before abandoning the car, he gave me detailed instructions on how to utilize a Desert Eagle gun. That is when I knew that something was wrong. He slowly got out of the car, walking towards the front, disappearing from my visibility. The event left me a bit confused and somewhat frightened of the possibility of something terrible occurring to either of us.

I looked around; there was no one in sight. For fifteen minutes I waited all alone in the car without any signs of danger. This all changed when a strange, all-white freight truck, not in the best of conditions, parked just a few feet in front of me. It was a bit concerning; however, the fact that I did not know what was going on was a key factor in helping me maintain my calm composure.

The truck driver, a man in his fifties with a somewhat unrefined appearance, emerged from his vehicle wearing a dusty white shirt, blue jeans, and brown work boots. Without hesitation, he made his way directly to the rear tires to inspect the air pressure. The middle-aged individual then retrieved his toolkit from the interior of the truck. The events unfolded at a languid pace, and I couldn't help but notice that my father was conspicuously absent.

The whole situation changed when a luxury black car

parked just a few feet behind me; this was the moment that made me become alert. I decided to duck down when I saw two mysterious men stepping out of the car. The fact that they parked right behind me made me think they were after us.

Both men, each clad in suits of varying light shades, passed by me without glancing into the car where I remained composed, acutely aware of my surroundings. Instead, they approached the truck driver. Initially, I suspected that the driver had summoned the men. However, the situation took a dark turn when the men in suits coldly shot the truck driver. One of the men proceeded to open the truck's rear container while the other fired another shot into the driver's body. The two men then moved the driver's lifeless form into the back of the truck. Afterward, one of them, whose identity I could not discern, drove away in the truck, while the other returned to the luxury car. A sense of foreboding lingered as one of the men peered through the window to check for any occupants inside. I instinctively held my breath and averted my gaze, wanting the man to leave as quickly as possible. The sound of the car engine gradually faded from the scene, and I decided to sit up in my seat and look around. The moment felt dull since there was an incredible amount of silence surrounding the area.

The entire situation was puzzling. Curiosity made me disregard my father's specific instructions. Therefore, I decided to exit the car in hopes of finding him nearby. I walked straight to the scene of the crime, but there was no evidence of blood or footprints on the floor. Things were unclear to me; therefore, there were many things I had to put some thought into.

A few moments later, I walked to the car and waited, believing that my father would return. However, a significant amount of time passed, and he was nowhere to be seen. I did not know where I was at, but that did not stop me from examining my situation and coming to the difficult conclusion that I had to leave. My age and lack of driving experience were hindering my progress. Nonetheless, it was essential that I depart from the scene.

With minimal practice, I drove north up the road, not knowing where I was heading. Luckily for me, we had stopped for gas a bit before that whole incident, although he had only filled the tank halfway. The window of opportunity opened when I saw a small two-floor motel. Something inside told me that the motel was a good place to stop. Drained from all the tension and the difficult decisions, I took a quick nap inside the car. I was fortunate that none of the personnel of the motel caught me.

It was an hour past noon by the time I woke up. From that hour all the way to nighttime, I secretly watched all the guests and the employees freely roam the grounds of the hotel. Unfortunately, I couldn't find any money inside the car, and I was both hungry and thirsty by four o'clock.

I decided to step out of the car. The area was clear; most of the housekeepers and maintenance staff had left the establishment. I searched for a water fountain where I could get some water for free. The significance of this action was immense, as it provided me with a more comprehensive comprehension of the dimensions and exits of the location. I was fortunate enough to find a water fountain by the pool. With caution, I headed back to the car to pick up my plastic water bottle. On my way, I was also able to locate where the janitors' office was. Once I filled my bottle of water, I headed back to my car, where I would wait patiently for the night to fall.

Since I was confident that the area was in good shape, I carefully stepped out of the car and walked straight to the janitor's room, where I was hoping to find the keys to the room I had carefully selected. To make sure nobody would see me, I looked in all possible directions, giving me the peace I needed to continue on. With a toothpick, I managed to unlock the janitors' door. Before this attempt, I had no experience unlocking a door with any type of object. I picked the key to the room from a wooden keyholder mounted on the wall. It was more convenient to sleep in one of the rooms on the bottom floor. I was lucky enough to have gone through the whole procedure unnoticed. After a peculiarly strange day, I headed to my room, which was across the hall, on the corner right, of the first floor. The stress of all the strange things that had happened to me made me lie down in bed and fall asleep shortly after.

I could barely guess what time it was, given it was fall and there wasn't really much sunlight. It took me around five minutes to rub my eyes and become fully aware of my surroundings. Something made me jump abruptly once I had full visibility. My father was sitting in the chair near the door. I was confused while being at a loss for words. He made matters worse by slowly clapping. I understand that I was only thirteen, but this was by far the strangest, yet the most remarkable thing that I have ever witnessed, given that he has never expressed feelings of satisfaction or approval for that matter.

"A brave soul you are, braver than I ever was. Today, you have made me a proud father."

Even though I was caught off guard by his compliment, it felt good knowing that my dad was proud of my decision-making abilities.

"Get up, and get ready; we still have not completed our journey," my father said while rising from his chair.

Being just a few minutes away from our destination, I had more questions than I did before. I decided to ask him one: "What is happening?"

I will never forget the smile he had on his face, nor his reply, "I'm not the one who should answer that question."

I remember we didn't make any eye contact.

"In time you will be the one to have all the answers," he said while driving through an illustrious orange and yellow leaf-covered forest.

We finally reached our destination. A mid-size, two-story cabin in the middle of the woods. No cars were around. It felt totally isolated, but I liked it, given what had happened to me in the last twenty-four hours. Matt, a gray-haired man in his seventies, wearing blue jeans and a striped shirt, came out of the cabin. My dad told me to stay in the car. He greeted the man with a warm hug before having a short conversation for about four minutes.

My father and I arrived at the cozy wooden cabin of perfectly well-placed logs. At the entrance, there was a large black bearskin rug on the floor. Despite the limited space available inside, the premise was meticulously decorated with items that one might expect to find in a hunting establishment. A magnificent deer head adorned with substantial antlers was prominently displayed on the right wall. The back wall had a large fireplace that stretched from the floor all the way to the ceiling. All of these things caught my attention, since I did not have much hunting knowledge.

Matt led us to two rooms situated on the second floor, traversing a wooden staircase that emitted an unusual sound. The rooms were right next to each other at a distance of about ten feet. My father and I agreed to take a break. To ease my mind from the challenging circumstances I encountered.

The sun was about to set, and I was helping the old

man carry some tree logs. My father was still in his room. It didn't worry me; I was enjoying my time with Matt. He lit the logs, and the fire rose slowly. Everything felt right. Matt sat next to me and gave me a marshmallow stick. I ate it as it was, which made him laugh, for some reason.

After some time and a few drinks, Matt was seemingly drunk, intending to scare me with some old folklore. I went on with it, however, because of my curiosity and willingness to learn something new. Halfway through one of his stories, a high-end Lexus, with a shiny silver color. Stopped at about fifty feet from the campfire. Matt abruptly slowed down and approached the men seated in the car. It was quite amusing how the old man's personality changed so rapidly. A slim, well-groomed man with dark hair stepped out of the driver's seat. Subsequently, an additional individual, possessing distinct physical attributes but exhibiting similar conduct, gradually departed from the passenger's seat.

I was ready to walk towards them, but my father stopped me, telling me to stay, which was precisely what I did. My dad and the man whom I did not know exchanged handshakes. They had a small conversation that I was unable to hear. Simultaneously, Matt gestured to the men to enter the cabin. Something out of the ordinary would happen, which was the fact that the second man who departed from the car shut all the curtains, blocking every chance I might have had to sniff out any piece of information. I waited long hours until my dad told me, "Charles, put out the fire and come over."

In the storage room, I grabbed a bucket and filled it with water from the faucet nearby. I threw the water over the fire, and it went off immediately. After putting the bucket back in the storage room, I walked towards the cabin, without a clue of what was going on.

Not knowing what the small reunion was about, I took a seat in front of my father, adjacent to the anonymous individual. Matt served me some hot chocolate, which had a uniquely delicious flavor. I was not certain of what Matt was cooking, but from the tasty smell, I came to the conclusion that he was making a soup for his guests.

"I apologize for keeping you out for so long, Charles; these are old friends of mine." I slightly nodded my head while asking myself why he had left me outside for around two hours.

"Now, tell me, young man, what would you like to do when you grow up?"

I answered, "I would like to work at a coffee shop."

There was a tense silence in the room, accompanied by the most ferocious gaze my dad had ever given me. I cooled off the situation, saying, "Just kidding! I would love to be an engineer."

The man next to me asked, "What type of engineer?"

"Maybe a mechanical engineer." I randomly said, not really knowing.

"Great choice!" the man sitting to the right of my father said.

All individuals, except my father, exhibited a serene and composed demeanor.

Matt came with two bowls of chicken noodle soup, along with a nice cold homemade tomato juice. Which he kindly placed in front of both men.

"Can I have this to go?" one of the men asked.

Matt replied, "Sorry, but I don't have any plastic containers for you to take it," Matt said.

"No problem. It's been wonderful visiting you, anyway," the men said as they rose from their chairs.

"Patrick, it's been great catching up with you," the men said to my dad once they were on their feet.

"The pleasure is mine, gentlemen."

My father excused himself from the table to formally bid farewell to the guests. Shortly thereafter, Matt emerged from the kitchen carrying a large container he had discovered at the back of the cabinet next to the sink. Unfortunately, by that time, the guests had already departed. With my father away, Matt and I savored the expertly prepared dinner in a quiet atmosphere, engaging in minimal conversation primarily focused on culinary topics. We concluded our meal with a slice of apple pie, which turned out to be even more delightful than the soup he had prepared earlier.

The following morning was cold yet pleasantly sunny, and I felt a sense of anticipation as I prepared to go fishing with my father. We got into our car and drove to a local fishing destination. Although it was moderately busy, we were fortunate to find a convenient parking spot.

We made our way to the service kiosk, where a friendly young lady assisted us. My father inquired about renting a small canoe along with two fishing rods. However, only one canoe and one fishing rod were available. My father, undeterred by the limitation, expressed that he was content simply accompanying me on the outing.

The young lady kindly assisted us by pushing the canoe into the water once we were settled inside. My father then began to paddle toward his favorite fishing spot. The autumn landscape surrounding us was exceptionally picturesque. As my father paddled, a group of kayakers swiftly glided past us, adding to the lively atmosphere of the morning.

As we continued, we encountered an elderly man with an unkempt appearance, holding a bucket. The scene could well have been part of a suspenseful film. My father turned to me and asked if I was interested in trying my hand at paddling. Naturally, I accepted the challenge and paddled for the first time.

I must admit that the experience turned out to be more difficult than I had anticipated, yet it was still quite enjoyable. After approximately ten minutes, my father instructed me to stop, and I complied.

"We have arrived," my father said.

The waters were calm, and the canoe rested motionless on the surface. My father stood while I remained seated, taking the opportunity to explain the fundamentals of fishing. Following his guidance, I put the bait onto the hook, turned my shoulder to generate momentum, and cast the line into the water, then settled in to await a bite. However, my lack of enthusiasm caused my interest to wane. My father, discerning my feelings, maintained confidence in my abilities and assured me that I would catch a fish before our outing concluded. His unwavering belief was reassuring, especially given my doubts. After another hour had passed unsuccessfully, I had a sudden inspiration. I decided to change the bait and seek a different location, hoping it would be more abundant with fish. Within just five minutes, I successfully caught my first fish—a beautiful white perch, as my father described. Observing his expression, I could see that he felt a profound sense of pride in my accomplishment.

"Shall we call it a day?" My father asked.

I was having a great time; therefore, I wanted to catch one more fish.

"Fine," he replied.

It took him only 20 minutes to catch a fish; the only difference was the color and size.

"I think we have gotten ourselves dinner, don't you think?"

"Yes." I agreed.

He gently rubbed my head while I smiled and put his fish next to mine. Looking at them together, the difference in size was embarrassing.

My dad paddled on. I was still amazed at the beauty of the lake. This time, we did not pass anyone; we only saw an old wooden cabin with a watermill, which was at a significant distance. The sight was pleasant at first but disturbing soon after. I saw an old lady lying on the ground.

With a discreet voice tone, I told my dad, To your right."

He did as I had asked him and replied, "What is wrong?" My father said, surprised to witness the strange scene.

"The lady near the watermill, she is on the ground."

Once my father saw the hopeless lady, he did not hesitate and paddled towards her. We reached the mill, where my dad ordered me to stay, which was the opposite of what I wanted to do. As always, I did as he said. I carefully took notice of my dad, who was on the ground near the woman's heart, checking her wrist. He waved me towards him, so I left the canoe and ran towards him.

"Check the house; see if you can find anything to help the woman."

I sprinted to the house, almost as if something good was happening.

There were rustic probes and wooden furniture in the cabin, as well as a wooden couch with faded and dirty fabric cushions. I went straight to the kitchen hoping to find a first aid kit, but I didn't see anything. I checked all the cabinets, but I couldn't find anything that could help the old lady. Without thinking twice, I entered the first bedroom I saw, but it was also empty, except for a badly arranged bed and a badly painted dresser with five drawers, one of which didn't close. Out of pure intuition, I looked everywhere, but there was nothing to find.

For a moment, I took a break to think things through. My father came just when I had given up, which was never a good thing. The sight of him made me stand up, but it didn't prevent him from snapping at me.

"What are you doing?"

I stared into his eyes and replied, "Sorry, I tried everything I could, but there is nothing in this house."

He confidently walked to the kitchen and opened all the counters like a madman. He then walked back to the front of the cabin to look through the fixed-pane window.

"Go to the room and lock the door, now," he shouted at me.

Being 13 years old has the big downside of not listening to your parents in the most crucial moments of life.

"Your life may be in danger if you don't—"

Before he could finish his sentence, a bullet flew in from the front window, breaking a ceramic ornament on the small living room table.

"Get down!" my father shouted.

Just as it happened, a torrent of bullets began to pierce the entire dwelling. This was probably the scariest moment in my life. One of those moments that live with you for the rest of your life. Interestingly, the bullets continued to penetrate the wooden walls of the cabin. My father looked around, trying to figure out what to do next. When the bullets stopped, he signaled me to carefully crawl to a safe spot. I was hesitant, and he knew it. He comforted me by grabbing my head and saying,

"We will do this together."

Those words were the confidence boost I needed to take action. I quickly crawled to the nearest room. I hit my knee on the way, but I was too afraid to look at any possible injuries. Pushing through the pain and fear was tough, but I had to do it if I wanted to live. Mostly out of fear, I was exhausted and trying my best to get through this nightmare. Finally, I got to the room. Bullets had barely touched that particular room. Therefore, I took a chance to peek through the window. I didn't see anything. Everything became more confusing when the bullets suddenly stopped. A few minutes later, I heard my father's footsteps entering the room.

"Are you alright?" My father asked.

I gave him a slight nod of my head before he gave me a hug.

"Let's get out of here," he said.

We walked together to the living room, which looked

like it had been in a war. However, what caught my attention was the fact that the old lady lying on the floor seemed somehow unharmed. This was a big surprise, given that she was totally unconscious. I stopped and told my father, "She may very well be alive." He was in front of me and near the door, his back facing me.

He turned around and said, "We tried to save this woman and almost got killed. I don't believe it is a good idea to help her."

As we were about to leave, I gave her one last look before taking a deep breath.

Back in the great outdoors, everything was as tranquil as ever, which was baffling to me, given what just occurred. It was strange to see a potentially life-threatening scenario for the first time, for some reason; nevertheless, I was happy with how I had dealt with the situation. My dad and I started paddling back to the kiosk after getting on the canoe. It was evident that we had not encountered any individuals, which was a significant relief. We neared the dock, where the lovely lady was waiting for us.

"How did it go?" the lady asked.

"Couldn't have gone better."

This was probably the most ironic thing that I'd heard my father say in all my life.

"How about you, young man?"

"I had a blast," I replied.

The lady helped both my dad and me step out of the

canoe.

A question lingered in my head: What had just happened back in the old lady's house?

Without needing to ask, my father said, "Don't tell anybody what happened; it can incriminate us."

"How? We didn't do anything," I replied, confused by my father's statement.

My dad slammed on the brakes hard, resulting in the car coming to a complete stop.

"We shall not speak of anything that has occurred. Do I make myself clear?"

I didn't dare to respond; instead, I nodded in agreement.

"Good," he said, and kept driving.

"I believe it's better if we go home," I suggested.

"We will not let bad luck ruin our time together."

Before returning to the cabin, we stopped at a restaurant that was tidy, inviting, and reasonably priced—a welcome combination. We chose a booth to settle into, and a waiter promptly approached to take our drink orders. My father requested a glass of cold water, while I ordered a strawberry milkshake, hoping that our visit would proceed without any unexpected occurrences. As I surveyed the establishment, my eyes were drawn to an antique jukebox, which piqued my curiosity, making it difficult to resist taking a closer look.

"Can I go see the jukebox?"

"Sure," my dad quickly replied.

I got up with great anticipation to look at the beautiful multicolored machine.

There were many songs I didn't know. This didn't stop me from asking my dad for some spare change. With pleasure, he gave me three coins, which were about seventy-five cents. There were countless songs, but I didn't know which one to pick. I saw the waitress pass by with my milkshake, so I picked a random song by Led Zeppelin and went back to my seat.

"Great choice," my father said.

I started sipping the milkshake, which was excellent. The waiter came to us after some time.

"Are you ready to order?"

"Yes, two cheeseburgers, please," my father replied.

"Right away." The waiter said.

The music was over, but I wasn't in the mood to ask my dad for more money. I faced my fear and gave it one more try.

"Father, may I choose one more song, please?"

He had a slight grin when he heard the question. He proceeded to give me the money anyway. I walked back to the jukebox to pick another song. I wanted to pick something new. While I was still deciding, the machine got stuck. It started functioning a few seconds later. It felt different this time and sounded a bit odd. All of a sudden, there were no more songs; instead, a message popped up on my screen, which read:

"Be careful who you trust."

It was strange and confusing, and I didn't know how to react. The jukebox picked a random song; luckily, it was by my dad's favorite band, The Beatles. I sat, and my father told me, "What a way to brighten my mood!"

After the song ended, the waiter came back with our food. He placed our food in front of both of us before saying, "Enjoy!"

We enjoyed our meal while engaging in various discussions. It was a memorable experience, particularly considering that I had not spent much quality time with my father before this outing. Both of us felt pleasantly full, to the point where we had no capacity for dessert. My father then requested the bill and settled our expenses in cash.

We left satisfied. I was worried, though. Something about this trip felt wrong; strange things had happened since it began. We were only a few miles away when two police officers stormed by us at opposite ends. My father didn't mind, of course. Finally, after a long and strange day, we were back at Matt's house. Nothing seemed off, even though my intuition was telling me that something was not right. Since it was a feeling, and I was not sure if I was right about what my mind was telling me, we simply entered the cabin.

"We are back!" My dad said, loudly, as we entered.

Not receiving a reply concerned both of us. My father would go on to grab a revolver concealed under the kitchen sink. He instructed me to wait. It was a weird déjà vu moment that I had experienced in real life. If there was something I'd learned on this trip, it was to be patient. I had no clue what was going on. All I heard was the sound of the top window suddenly shattering. Quickly, my father ran up the stairs, but by the time he reached the window of his room, the man who had caused this unfortunate situation had left. It did not take him long to walk down the stairs, where I was patiently sitting at.

"Are you ok?"

"Yes," I replied without any hesitation.

"What about Matt?" I asked since I was worried about him

"He is not home."

"Shall we call the police, then?"

My father was placing the revolver back under the kitchen counter when he answered, "No, we just wait."

"What about the man who sneaked into the house?"

My father poured himself a glass of Scotch whiskey, while I asked, worried, about the possible dangers that I could be facing.

"Forget that he exists," my dad said, not nearly as concerned as I was.

I felt the need to clear my mind of things. Therefore, I decided to head outside, which was probably not the best decision, due to all the odd circumstances. While outside,

I found a book that was in solid condition, although it did look a bit dated.

The title of the book was Gone with the Wind. At that age, I was not into reading, but I decided to give it a try. I finished the first chapter, and I kept going because it actually was quite interesting. My attention shifted 20 pages into the second chapter after I saw a police car park in front of the cabin. My father was already at the door before I even had the chance to call him. The officer was on duty, fully uniformed. Matt had gotten out of the passenger seat. The officer greeted my dad and said, "Looks like your friend got a little lost there."

"No worries, I will handle it," my dad replied.

The officer departed shortly thereafter, while my father directed Matt to the bathroom.

After my father finished assisting Matt, he came downstairs to have some leftover soup from the previous day.

"What is wrong with him?" I asked my dad while he was enjoying his soup.

"He is just drunk."

I kept eating, and we didn't mention him for the rest of the night.

After some time, I sat at the living room table, waiting for my dad, who was washing both of our bowls.

Once finished, he said that we weren't able to play cards, since he considered that we both needed some rest.

With a feeling of dissatisfaction, I walked towards my

room, only to find a few bloodstains on the floor. I called my father, who came up immediately. He started to look around. It was a pattern leading to the bathroom. We both headed towards the bathroom, where Matt was lying in the bathtub with a cut on his right foot and an old book in his hand. From the looks of it, he had somehow cut his foot on the way to get the book that was missing from his shelf.

"Help me out," my father said.

We both tried to get Matt out while he was being quite annoying, constantly refusing our help. After trying a million times, we finally got him to calm down. My father grabbed him by the arms, while I grabbed him by the legs. We managed to get him out of there and drag him into his room upstairs and placed him on the bed. My dad took a huge, deep breath, given the amount of energy it took.

"Go on, I'll take it from here."

I walked back to my room tired, so worn out that I didn't even put on my pajamas to sleep.

The sound of a door knock woke me in the morning. My father opened the door and said, "Rise and shine."

I still hadn't gotten over the two days I'd had. I gazed out the window and was astonished by the magnificent panorama of a forest during autumn. A few seconds later, I went down to where my dad and Matt were eating breakfast.

"Join us," Matt said.

I sat next to him. It was astonishing the difference a

night can make. I drank the orange juice that was in front of me and started eating some scrambled eggs. My father was almost done and ready to take me to the next adventure. He left the table and stood by the door while Matt and I continued to eat our breakfast.

Matt had his mouth somewhat full when he asked, "What happened to me yesterday?"

I wanted to play off the situation, so I said, "You just had a bit too much to drink, that is all."

"Hard to get by when you are retired," Matt answered.

My father had gone upstairs after standing at the door for a few minutes. I completed my breakfast and washed both the plates and glass cups in a gesture of courtesy towards Matt, even though he was not paying attention.

I just sat on the bed, wondering, not knowing where or what would happen next. It was all a great adventure for me.

The sky was clear, and the breeze was gentle. We were driving south, with the windows down because I had requested it. A few minutes passed before my dad made a right and headed straight, following a sign that said, "Cameron Lake."

I was so happy that it was going to be a relaxing day. We stepped out of the car and grabbed our backpacks from the rear seat. We walked for around seven minutes before reaching the most beautiful lake I had ever seen. The spot was empty, which meant that I would at last find peace in a setting that I admired.

We threw our backpacks carelessly. The water was at the perfect temperature. I swam freely to warm my body up. My father, on the other hand, sat next to the backpacks watching me enjoy myself. After relaxing for a while, I wanted some company, so I called him at a distance.

"Come on in, the water is great!" I said, with an enthusiastic tone.

He was hesitant at first, but he eventually made up his mind. He took off his shirt and jumped into the water without testing the temperature first. My dad swam underwater like a fish. He stopped a few feet from where I was; he continued to amaze me with all of his wonderful skills.

"Why don't you try holding your breath for two minutes?" My dad suggested.

"You must be joking," I replied.

"No, I'm not."

I knew I would fail, but I still wanted to try anyway. So, I squeezed my nose and dove into the water. I shut my eyes and skipped counting, knowing that it would only add to my stress. I did my best to hold my breath for as long as I could manage. On my way out, I splashed my father with water. Luckily, he was not too bothered.

"Hum… 45 seconds is not bad, but I believe you can hold your breath for a minute and a half."

I stared at him as if he were speaking gibberish.

"Take a deep breath and meditate for 3 minutes."

I closed my eyes and cleared my mind of any distractions. After my time was up, I told my dad that I was going to do it.

"Whenever you are ready."

I tried again. This time I was more determined than the last time. I went back underwater and cleared my mind. I stopped holding my breath when I thought that I had achieved my goal. My father stared at me in disbelief of what I had accomplished.

"Exactly two minutes," announced my father.

Although he did not verbally express it, I could sense my father's pride in my achievements. We spent an additional hour in leisure before wrapping up our day. My father was the first to exit the area, while I lingered a bit longer, wishing to swim for a short while before leaving. After a brief swim, I took a few moments to enjoy some quiet solitude. It was then that I suddenly noticed my father's absence—he was nowhere to be found. Concerned, I promptly exited the water and made my way toward the tree where we had left our backpacks.

The fog started to gather around me. I took a deep breath and started walking around the forest. Birds flew over me, nothing unusual. However, what was unusual was the strange sound I heard, almost as if someone were playing an instrument. I finally arrived at the car, but my father wasn't there. I looked at the ground to see if there were any footprints, but there were none. The only thing that I had left to do was try to locate where that odd noise was coming from.

Slowly, I walked towards it. I was annoyed, since I despised walking barefoot. The source from which the noise was coming surprised me: it was a radio playing some type of instrumental music. I hid and waited to see what would happen. After half an hour, the radio started losing its frequency. A man approached, the same man fishing at the lake. He had a hunting rifle and a camouflage suit. I decided to follow him out of curiosity. He walked for around two miles before leading me to a tent. I stopped and headed back to the lake.

Countless thoughts roamed around my head. Halfway to the car, I ran into my dad.

"Where did you go?"

I wasn't in the mood to respond, but I had to. So I told him, "I thought I had lost you."

"No, I had gone to the car to put our backpacks away," my father said before adding, "Let's go."

In the living room of the cabin, we had a game of cards. He would beat me most of the time, but I didn't mind because I was enjoying it. He had finally taught me how to play poker, which was on my bucket list of things I wanted to learn. In the middle of one of the games, he taught me the importance of managing my money and how I shouldn't gamble if I didn't have enough money to pay my bills. This was hard for me to grasp at first, but it was important that I learned at a young age.

His phone rang suddenly; he got up and abandoned the game. I stayed there, examining the game while he spoke on the phone in the kitchen. He was done after six minutes; he didn't come back with good news.

"Grandad is feeling ill; I have to go check on him."

This was sad news because I thought our vacation had ended.

"It is just for a day; I will be back."

My father gave me a kiss on the forehead and left the house.

Matt was nowhere to be found, so that meant I had the house all to myself. I watched my dad leave quickly. Having time for myself was good and bad. I was in a cabin in the middle of the woods. It did not take long for me to turn on the old TV in the living room. I ended up incredibly disappointed that I could not find anything that would fit my taste in television.

I turned it off and headed outside, hoping to find something that would keep me busy. The storage room caught my eye, thinking there might be something interesting in there.

The room was dimly lit and densely packed with various items, emanating an unusual odor. Upon switching on the light, I discovered that its illumination barely penetrated the cluttered space, revealing a considerable accumulation of neglected objects. I navigated the area with caution, mindful of potential hazards hidden beneath my feet. As I surveyed the surroundings, nothing initially piqued my interest—until my gaze fell upon an old bicycle that appeared to be the perfect size for me.

I made my way back to the cabin's front porch to remove the layers of dust that had settled on the bicycle, which occupied my attention for quite some time. Noticing that the tires were low on air, I returned to the storage room to retrieve an old air pump, which, fortunately, was still functional. Moments later, I decided to clean the bicycle, as it had clearly not been maintained for some time and required a thorough dusting.

I grabbed my backpack and walked towards the road. I looked at both sides, left and right. With much anticipation, I got on the bicycle and started riding north. The feeling of the cold breeze behind me was a pleasant one. I maintained a steady pace while riding in the bike lane situated at the side of the road. I arrived at the small town filled with different stores.

Fortunately for me, there was a bike rack where I could park my bike. Once my bike was tightly locked to the rack, I continued my journey on foot. I took out a large coat from my backpack because I had started to feel a bit cold. There were many great shops, restaurants, and a small park nearby. However, what really stood out to me was a fountain with a beautiful Roman statue. The silence of the environment covered all my senses, plunging me into an immense inner peace. Just a few steps away from the fountain was a bench, where I sat to better enjoy the incredible ambience.

Everything came to an end when a group of rowdy protesters marched on the street. They were passive at first but, eventually, turned aggressive, disturbing the beautiful peace of the town.

Thankfully, the sheriff arrived with the light bar on. The people were in complete disregard of the authorities' presence.

The police officer got out of his car and walked towards the protesters to try to calm down the situation, although they would not yield to the law. One of the protesters told the officer to leave. Obviously, the policeman held his ground and refused to listen to the illogical request.

Things got very tense when one of the protesters pulled out a gun. This was the deciding factor for the officer to pull that man out of the crowd, eventually arresting him. I left the scene, not wanting to be part of what was going on. On my way to the bike rack, I ran into a rather intriguing Chinese restaurant; I unzipped my bag to check if I had enough money to buy myself a meal.

The place was clean and well-kept. A young Chinese woman, standing by the wooden counter with long, well-groomed hair and a peculiar perfume of fresh flowers, kindly welcomed me inside.

"Just you?"

I was so young that I was afraid to reply. Although, I eventually said yes.

She led me to a table near a fish tank filled with multicolored fish. I sat down and placed my backpack next to me. A strange silence surrounded the restaurant, which was quite surprising as it was almost lunch hour. A middle-aged Chinese man approached.

"What would you like to drink?"

"Just a glass of cold water, please."

"Right away," the waiter replied.

The beautiful Chinese paintings on the wall caught my eye. They said so much about a place I'd always wanted to visit. I looked around and started working on a crossword puzzle on the table. This was a fun activity that kept me busy while I waited for the waiter. The man came back with my water.

"Are you ready to order?" the waiter asked.

"Just give me five more minutes to think."

"Sure," the waiter replied.

I was indeed ready but wanted to stay a bit longer to make up time before I returned to the cabin. I took a sip of water and continued playing with my crossword puzzle. The front door kept opening and closing, which probably meant that there were more people coming into the restaurant. Even though I enjoyed the emptiness of my surroundings, I was happy to know that the restaurant had the recognition that it deserved. The waiter was walking towards me. I took notice of the dull expression on his face. Nonetheless, I wished to refrain from being too indiscreet and glancing at his new clients in the rear. His mood had changed from being happy to being disheartened.

"Are you ready, young man?" He asked in a very polite manner, even though his mood had changed.

"I'll have the sweet and sour chicken with white rice and mixed vegetables, please."

"Right away," he replied.

He left with the menu towards the kitchen. A spark of curiosity lit up inside me. I knew that it was still too early for me to turn around and look at the people who had just entered the restaurant. My attention had shifted to trying to identify the people who were talking. They called the lady in the front and started to speak in Chinese. Maybe they owned the place, and that is what had caused my waiter's mood to swing. Moved by my curiosity, I asked an employee for the bathroom.

"Straight down, to the right."

"Ok, thanks."

I headed towards the bathroom, which was quite chilly inside. I didn't have the intention to use the restroom. The door opened within a minute of me being there. This can't be happening, I said to myself. The man, who was wearing all-black, polished, formal shoes, used the stall two doors down. My sixth instinct told me to wait for him to leave, most likely because I didn't know who the man was. It took him around thirty seconds to finish and flush the toilet. He then went to wash his hands. This took him another thirty seconds, but the loud ring of his phone interrupted him. He started speaking in Chinese, so I didn't understand.

His voice sounded similar to that of the man who was behind me. The conversation went on for around another 15 minutes before he left. I felt like a kid in a candy store. To not make it seem obvious, I remained sitting on top of the toilet for another five minutes before I got out of the bathroom.

Walking back, I felt something was different. I turned right back to my table and couldn't believe my eyes; all the beautiful paintings had been removed and replaced with pictures of Chinese architecture! I paused in disbelief and rubbed my eyes to make sure that I wasn't dreaming. Why would they do that? I asked myself. The place was totally unrecognizable. The plate of food that I had ordered was at the table, and my backpack was still there, which was important to me. I took a sip of water. The plate of food was as appetizing as I could have imagined. I took the first bite, and it made my mouth water.

The meal was even better than the soup that Matt had cooked. A group of old people sat beside me. I was done with my principal plate. The waiter came to my table short-ly after.

"Would you like anything for dessert?"

"No, thanks," I replied. But he insisted.

"Why don't you look at our menu to see if there is something you would like? I'll come back."

I read the menu, but nothing caught my eye. He took the drinks order from the table next to me before coming back.

"Did something interest you?"

"No, thanks," I replied.

"No problem," said the waiter before taking the menu away. He quickly brought me my bill with a fortune cookie.

"Whenever you are ready."

I took my time and ate the fortune cookie first. I don't believe too much in fortune, but I read it anyway. The message said, A long journey awaits. What can that possibly mean? I took out the exact 11 dollars my meal cost from the front pocket of my backpack and put them on the tab. The waiter arrived shortly and took the tab to the registrar. He was going to bring me the change, but I refused due to the good service.

"Have a good day and come back anytime," he said as I was getting ready to leave.

I put on my jacket before happily walking out of the restaurant.

The outside looked different from when I went in. The delicious food occupied my stomach in a way it had not done in a long time. I spotted a white bench next to a small wedding shop, where I decided to take a seat.

The streets were calm, except for the construction

workers who worked diligently on their craft. I was content with how my day had gone until this point. It had given me the space I needed to relax. I put my backpack on my lap and closed my eyes for about five minutes. It was not until I felt the presence of someone sitting next to me that I woke up. I looked right to greet them. I remembered his face. It was one of the men from the protest.

I didn't like to speak to strangers, but I couldn't help but ask,

"Excuse me, sir, what was the motive behind the protest earlier?"

"Lousy investors buying land," he kindly answered.

I had no idea what he meant.

"What do you mean, sir?"

"The people who are buying the land are not particularly good people," he added, hesitantly, not wanting to give me a more profound explanation.

The situation was tense and awkward. This was enough for me to decide to stand up and leave the bench.

Walking back to where my bicycle was, I heard the voice of a drunk man shouting for help. The fact that there were many people around and no one would pay attention made me believe that I was hearing voices in my head. I approached the closed sewer the voice was coming from. It did not take long for me to take off the circular top of the sewer.

"PLEASE HELP!" A gritty old man shouted.

I looked around, assessing my options. The construction workers were working hard, undisturbed. The situation was delicate, and the old man in the sewer needed assistance. I interrupted them to explain what was going on. Fortunately, the men, who looked quite exhausted from their job, were understanding enough to examine the situation.

The fact that the workers witnessed what I saw with my own eyes confirmed that I was not going crazy at all. The men called an ambulance immediately, which arrived in a matter of minutes. The paramedics asked the man multiple times to climb the stairs, but for some reason, he did not pay attention. They asked if I could go down and try to convince him to come up. Even though I found everything to be odd, I did not hesitate to try to assist the man.

Taking the dark, narrow steps was frightening. I eventually got to the bottom, where the old man, with crooked teeth and greasy gray hair, asked me if I had come to save him from his misery. From the way he looked and spoke, I could tell he was incoherent.

"Is everything okay?" One of the paramedics asked.

"No, he doesn't seem to be in the right state of mind," I answered.

"Is he injured?"

I took a good look at the man, but he did not seem to have any injuries of any sort.

"No, he does not appear to be."

"Fine, come back up. We will handle this ourselves."

I climbed back to the top, where the paramedics and construction workers had gathered. One of the main paramedics extended my hand.

"You have done a heck of a job. And for that, you have all my respect."

After all the unusual things that had occurred, I walked back to my bicycle, still at the same place that I had left it. I unlocked it and left the village with mixed feelings. Riding my bicycle was a good way to keep my mind off things. The road back was empty, which I was grateful for. However, it was getting windy, and the clouds were looking really dark. I pedaled a bit faster, wanting to avoid the hard rain that was about to fall.

I was advancing quickly, and the traffic remained low. On my way, I came across a group of deer with their newborn fawn crossing the road. I halted my movements as I apprehensively avoided provoking them, as this was my initial encounter with wild deer passing by casually. Cold drops of rain began to pour down. It felt more like a tranquilizer than anything else. I decided to ride slower to avoid any incidents.

As the heavy rain began to subside, I made my way onto the dirt road that led to the cabin. Although the precipitation had ceased, my gray pants had become soiled, prompting thoughts of a refreshing shower and the comfort of my cozy bed—a welcome respite from the events of the day. Suddenly, from a few miles away, I detected the distinct odor of gasoline. To my dismay, I realized that the shed where I had discovered the bicycle was engulfed in flames. Without hesitation, I abandoned the bicycle and sprinted towards Matt's house.

"Quick, we need some water! Your shed is on fire!"

He laughed it off.

"I'm not joking, your shed is burning."

He then went on to reply, "It's just an experiment."

I couldn't tell if he was being delusional or if he was being honest.

"Let's go, I'll show you."

Skeptically, I followed him towards the shed. The fire was still there even though there was no smoke.

"It's for the bears, but it does not seem to be working."

Matt designed and installed a specialized tube system, which he constructed himself, asserting his background as an engineer with expertise in creating unconventional devices. The system was engineered to deter various animals, including bears. Instead of relying solely on flames for deterrence, the primary mechanism involved the strong odor emitted by the flames, which served to repel the bears effectively.

And just like that, he entered the shed, and the fire went away. He came back outside and removed a metal tube mounted on the corner. He showed it to me before mounting it back on the side of the shed. What a great idea it was. Matt, who came out of the shed with binoculars wrapped around his neck, locked the door.

"Follow me," he said.

In between the trees, he was leading the way. We walked for around fifty feet until we stopped by a stream.

"Sit down, there is something that you might want to see."

I sat down, and in about 10 minutes, a group of brown bears arrived near the stream. It was astonishing to see various groups of bears fishing in the stream.

"Here, take a look," Matt said while handing me his binoculars.

Through the binoculars, I had a better look at what the bears were doing.

"Shall we go now?" Matt asked.

I stopped looking through the binoculars before nodding and heading back towards the cabin.

When Matt and I arrived at the cabin, a log fire was set. We were both concerned as to who could have set up this fire. The creepy old man I had seen at the park came out from behind the shed.

"Stay back, I'll handle it," Matt told me.

"What on Earth do you think you are doing here?"

The man completely omitted his presence. Matt was infuriated. He went to his shed to grab an old-school revolver. Once, outside, he began to recklessly shoot into the air. In little to no time, the man ran away from the scene.

Matt then returned to his shed, where he would put back his revolver. Just as he was exiting the shed, a police car arrived at the scene. Both Matt and I shared the same look of confusion once the police officer got out of his car.

"Put your hands up, right now!"

"What is the issue, officer?"

The police officer was extremely mad and did not answer his question. He instead proceeded to shoot at Matt numerous times before leaving.

My heart broke to see that a man like Matt met his death in such a lewd way. I took my shirt off to help stop the bleeding.

"Stay with me, Matt."

He rubbed his hand on my face and said, "Your father loves you, Charles. One day, you will become an important man.

Slowly, Matt began to close his eyes until he met his final destiny. I lay on the floor, saddened and in great disbelief.

It was the hardest moment I had faced until this point. I waited next to Matt until my father arrived in his car. He noticed from a significant distance away, and he rushed out with a gun in hand.

"What happened?" My father asked.

"A police officer came and shot Matt."

My father looked around, aiming his gun in different directions. He asked me to remain where I was. I followed his order while he sprinted into the cabin.

"Come in, it's fine," my dad said, after making sure the interior of the cabin was safe.

I was in great emotional pain. My father prepared me a sandwich and put it on the table along with some hot chocolate. I wasn't in the mood, however, and he took notice.

"Eat, I need you to help me bury the body."

I looked at him as if he were a lunatic.

"We need to do it, out of respect for him," my father said, knowing that his request was not easy for me to do.

I went on to eat my sandwich and drink my hot chocolate. My saddened father walked out of the cabin. He was deeply impacted by the loss of Matt; seeing him affected was something difficult to watch. I kept eating to calm myself down, but even that was challenging to do.

Outside, my father was digging a hole. I grabbed a shovel near him to give him a helping hand. The hole was deep, at least my father thought so, as he signaled me to stop.

"Let's get the body in."

My father climbed back to the top while I waited for him to help me out. I shook off the dirt on my shirt and pants. We carried Matt to the hole and threw him inside. I stood carefully looking at my father staring at Matt. He then turned around.

"Go back inside; your job is finished."

By this time, it was already midnight, and all I wanted to do was to take a long shower.

After my long shower, I went straight to my room and put my pajamas on. I looked out of the window and saw that the hole my father and I had dug had been completely covered up. My father came into the room and suddenly said, "Pack your things; we are leaving."

After changing into regular clothes, I took one last look at the room before shutting the door. Coming down the stairs, the strong odor of gasoline worried me a bit. It was my dad who was pouring gasoline all over the cabin. Once he saw me, he told me, "Wait for me in the car."

I walked straight to the car and sat in the passenger seat. My father continued pouring until there was no more gas left in the gasoline tank. He took a lighter out of his pocket and lit the whole place up. My eyes couldn't believe what I was seeing. My father walked towards me, smelling a bit like gasoline. He started the car and immediately left.

"Are we going back home?" I asked my father.

"Give me your water bottle."

I handed him the water that I had in my backpack. He was so thirsty that he almost drank the entire bottle.

"We need to make one more stop," he said. Which was not the answer I was hoping for, since all I wanted to do was to go home.

By the time I woke up, we were already at our destination. A beautifully illuminated town with an eternal winter vibe.

"You woke up just in time," my father said.

He kept driving for another five miles before he stopped on the side of the road next to a valet parking podium. A young man, wearing jeans and a thick fur coat, opened the door for me and my father.

"Grab your stuff."

I got my backpack from the back and got out of the car. Shortly after, another man wearing similar attire came to pick us up in a white van.

We left the town behind to get on a highway, which led us to a luxurious five-star ski resort. The man stopped just outside the lobby. The driver stepped out and kindly opened the door for both my father and me.

"Enjoy, gentlemen," the driver remarked as my father handed him a generous tip for his exemplary service. As we entered the resort, a courteous doorman graciously held the door open for us. Upon stepping inside, I was captivated by the stunning luxury of the resort's interior, where elegant chandeliers cast a warm glow over the beautifully appointed furnishings. The air was infused with a pleasant aroma that I found difficult to pinpoint, but to me, it resembled a delightful blend of vanilla and pineapple. My senses were so enchanted by the surroundings that I found myself less concerned with the exact scent. A gracious attendant welcomed us with refreshing glasses of lemonade, which we gladly accepted before proceeding toward the reception area.

"How may I help you today, gentlemen?" A young man asked.

"I have a reservation."

"What name is it, sir?"

"Patrick."

"Yes, I believe everything is set. Enjoy your stay."

We walked towards the end of the hall to get the elevator. The interior of the light-brown and gold elevator was as impressive as the lobby. We got quickly to the seventh floor.

Finally, we could relax and watch TV in our room.

"Do you want to relax or go skiing tomorrow?"

I thought about it and decided that skiing was a way of relaxing. Therefore, I did not hesitate to give him a response.

My father took a deep breath and said, "Good choice, Charles." My proud dad said, before turning around and falling asleep.

We were having a late breakfast, given that we had gone to bed almost at three in the morning. Before going skiing, I had scrambled eggs with bacon and two slices of bread. My father, on the other hand, had a small glass of orange juice. I took my time. I was happy and had almost moved on from what had happened, but my father was quite the opposite. Something was wrong; I could tell from the blank look on his face. Since I was so eager to go skiing, I had not put too much thought into trying to figure out why he was concerned; I instead finished my food, since I was eager to go skiing.

"All done," I announced.

"Let's have some fun then," he replied.

As I ascended in the ski lift, I was enveloped by a panoramic vista of majestic mountains draped in a pristine blanket of fresh snow. The sight was both exhilarating and intimidating, each moment heightening my anticipation as the landscape unfurled beneath me. After what felt like an exhilarating eternity, the lift finally descended, and we disembarked, the crisp mountain air invigorating my senses as I strapped on my ski blades. The slope before me loomed steeply, promising an exhilarating rush. Before making my descent, my father offered a reassuring reminder to follow his lead. I acknowledged him with a nod, ensuring my helmet was securely fastened—a crucial step as I prepared to embrace the thrill that awaited me.

Adrenaline started pumping. I was going down the slope at an incredibly high pace. It was quite enjoyable until we reached the very end. My father stopped, and I did the same. He looked around, but I couldn't tell what it was that he was looking at.

"What is it?" I asked my father. He took a brief pause before answering, "Just follow me."

We continued our journey through a different route, which led us to a group of skiers. I didn't have a clue who these men were, but it wasn't my concern; all I wanted to do was enjoy my time with my father.

The man wearing a white-and-green attire asked my father, "Are you sure about this, Patrick?" My father nodded, while I stood confused.

"Son, these are the men that will make you untouchable. They will train you to become invincible, but only if you agree to go with them."

My mood suddenly changed; I took one more look at the men.

"Will you come with me?" He looked back at the men before looking at me once more.

"No, but please, accept their training, not only for you but for the people whom you most love."

I was empty, but somehow, I knew that I was doing the right thing. I looked at the men and said, "It will be an honor to receive your training."

I gave my dad one last hug before I left with the men.

CHAPTER 2

TRAINING

My first day was far from easy. The three enigmatic men, whom my father had instructed me to accompany, deprived me of my sight with an all-black mask, making the journey more distressing than it otherwise might have been. After approximately two hours, the vehicle came to a full stop. One of the men opened the door to my left and removed my mask, revealing an impressive four-story mansion adorned with expansive glass windows before me. The man gestured for me to walk alongside him as we approached the grand double doors made of solid maple. He utilized a sophisticated biometric lock, and I watched in fascination as the door opened automatically. The man, whose name remained unknown to me at that moment, kindly motioned for me to enter.

Crossing the threshold was akin to stepping into a neoclassical palace. The marble floors were so polished that they reflected my image, enhancing the sense of opulence surrounding me. It was still daylight, and the interior was suffused with natural light streaming through the numerous windows, rendering artificial illumination unnecessary. We ascended the staircase into one of the spacious rooms, where a man in his late forties, possessing a robust physique and dark hair, gazed thoughtfully out of a colossal window.

"Sir," the man beside me said.

The identity of the man observing from the window remained unknown to me at that time. Following the conclusion of my training, I ascertained that he was a leading figure in Canadian society, potentially placing him among the most powerful individuals worldwide. "My apologies, you are free to go."

The Canadian member bowed his head before leaving us alone.

"Charles, take a seat; make yourself at home."

I did as I was told, since I wanted to make a good impression.

"I'm truly delighted to have you here. What about you? How have the last couple of days been for you?"

"They have been... different, sir."

"Different in what way, young man?"

The man stared at my face with his cold gray eyes.

"They have tested my character, sir."

"How have you coped with the situation?" the man asked firmly.

"I believe I have dealt with it the best way I can," I answered.

"I believe so, too," the authoritative man said.

"Charles, your father put you through very difficult tests. Most people your age could not have handled what you have handled. This and many more reasons make you eligible for our training; however, we will not oblige you to do it."

I stopped for a moment to make the best choice.

"My father, why does he want me to do this?" I asked because I was aware that my father wouldn't provide an answer to such a question.

"He has his motives, but that should not influence your personal decision," the man said.

"If my father went through all this trouble to get me here, then you can be sure I want to complete the training."

The man pressed the bell on his table before replying.

"My man will take you to your training center. I wish to see you in a couple of years as a more... defined man."

The man who had led me to the leader entered the room.

"Please, take Charles to the training facility," the leader said from a short distance from where I was.

We walked out of the mansion to head directly into one of the many luxury cars that were parked on the side of the house.

The journey to my intended destination was not comparable to the previous one. The man took a turn on a road that led to a cypress wooden cabin. The surroundings reminded me of those at Matt's house. At that moment, I started wondering if Matt's death had been part of my training.

"Follow me," said the driver while stepping out.

The man and I walked inside the cabin without knocking on the door. Everything was well arranged, the floors were clean, and there was a natural scent of oranges, which made the house very pleasing. The driver called for my supposed trainer, shouting, Hello! Five minutes later, a man just over his fifties walked in, followed by a thin boy with a good physique.

"It looks like I have a new trainee," the trainer stated.

"Yes, Charles has accepted the training."

"I will take it from here, then," the trainer replied to the man who had driven me to the location.

The young, handsome man offered me his hand.

"Welcome, my name is Liam."

"Nice to meet you."

"Let me show you where you will stay."

Liam walked among the colossal trees of the forest. In my head, I was trying my best to get ready for wherever

I was going to be sleeping. After a short walk, we arrived at a small tent where I will stay for the rest of my training.

"Don't worry, your body will eventually get used to it." Liam told me, most likely judging by the expression on my face.

After his encouraging words, he grabbed a towel along with some spare clothes from the inside of the tent before leaving the area.

Upon entering the tent, I sought to assess its dimensions more closely. The interior was somewhat confined, with a sleeping bag, an inflatable mattress, two flashlights, bottles of water, several snacks, and a few berries occupying the space. The limited resources prompted me to reconsider my decision to participate in the training. However, despite its small size, the tent exuded a sense of comfort and coziness. After exiting, I looked around to determine if there were any tasks requiring my attention, but I found neither Liam nor the trainer present. I remained seated on the ground for an extended period, yet there were no signs of either individual. Although I felt inclined to explore the surrounding forest, I was reluctant to risk compromising my reputation on the first day. As evening approached, I decided to make my way toward the cabin, hoping to find the trainer awaiting my arrival. Upon reaching the cabin, I noted its desolate atmosphere, with no one in sight, and I refrained from entering, particularly given the dim lighting. It wasn't long before I returned to the tents, where I encountered Liam, who appeared to have just taken a shower, standing outside his tent.

"Is there something I need to do?" I asked Liam, not knowing what my duty was.

"No. The training will commence tomorrow. Have some rest; you are going to need it," Liam said before entering his tent.

I followed his advice, and therefore I entered the tent to get ready for the following day.

The unpleasant sound of an air horn was the rude awakening that woke me up the following morning. Liam opened my tent.

"Get up, we have work to do."

Even though it was my second day, it was officially my first day of training. I changed faster than a beam of light to make sure that Liam and my trainer knew that I was here to follow their training schedule.

Both Liam and the trainer were waiting to take me to a military-style training course. I would need to complete it daily until I finished my training. The obstacle course was long and exhausting. Liam took on the fierce course.

"A good start to the day begins with a good exercise. Each day you will do more and more laps," the trainer said. "Now, do you have any questions?"

"No, sir," I replied.

"Good, then, you shall begin."

The trainer went on to sit on a chair a few feet away

from me.

I thought about stretching out before commencing my training, but I didn't, as Liam had already started. The first obstacle I took on was two rows of wheels. This obstacle tested one's footwork and endurance. This was not the hardest of tasks. Nonetheless, it did possess a learning curve. Luckily for me, I was able to tackle the task fairly easily.

The subsequent task involved a lengthy ladder supported by two robust wooden posts, each approximately thirty feet in height. Although I was aware that this challenge would be considerable, I approached it with a sense of confidence. Exercising caution, I carefully ascended the ladder, ultimately reaching the top—a feat that elicited a profound sense of accomplishment.

After my small accomplishment, I would encounter monkey bars, which should be one of my strengths, since I loved to do them at the park when I was younger and a bit smaller. There were exactly twenty bars. The trainer had instructed me to do five pull-ups on each bar. This is where the big test began for me.

Liam was completing every obstacle with great ease, while my struggles continued. As Liam was about to overlap me, he told me the only way to fight through the pain was to forget it existed. His words were pivotal for me to stimulate my brain to finish the task.

The monkey bars were not as simple as I initially believed they would be, nonetheless. I managed to finish them. Without taking a breather, I had to swim 200 meters in a pool that was part of our daily training.

The next exercise was not difficult at all. However, because of my lack of training and the excessive nature of the exercise, I could not feel my arms. I had to lift a heavy tire from one end to another. But in the middle of each flip, I was required to do ten push-ups. Upon completion of this exercise, I was unable to feel my hands or legs.

I experienced an unfamiliar sensation, one I had never encountered before. Although I was neither overweight nor out of shape for my age, the intensity of this training regimen was unlike anything I had previously undertaken. I found myself facing one final challenge: traversing a rope from one end to the other without the use of my hands. This obstacle's complexity required complete focus, regardless of the fatigue one might be experiencing. Should I fail and fall into the mud pit, the consequence would entail an arduous set of three hundred jumping jacks followed by one hundred squats, after which I would be required to start the exercise anew.

Before the formidable challenge, I closed my eyes and counted to thirty. With my remaining energy reserves, I crossed the obstacle course. Although I had completed the course, I was instructed to repeat all the exercises several more times until the trainer's whistle commanded us to halt.

Liam came to ask how I was. I was reluctant to disclose my fatigue to him; however, after enduring a grueling two-hour training session, I was forced to tell him what my state of fatigue was.

After taking a much-needed break in the tent, we went back to the cabin. Liam and I sat at the maple wooden table in the living room. The trainer came from the kitchen and asked Liam to explain to me what the purpose of the training was while he set up the back room.

"You are here to train your mind and your body. Every day is a test; everything must be done the right way if you wish to complete the training."

Liam proceeded to lecture me on the importance of geography, a subject that more often than not gets overlooked.

Once he finished, he asked me to take a quick break before our next activity. Our time was up; therefore, Liam and I walked into the back room, where the trainer had set up two wooden desks. He arrived shortly and rolled down a map of the Americas.

"As members, we must know our locations. We have private investments all around the globe. Most times, we send young men just like you for two reasons. One, because you will not be spotted by the society of the country you are sent to. And two, to make sure the other societies are honest to their roles as members."

"Do all the societies do this, sir?" Liam wanted to

know if all the countries had the same form of operating.

"All the societies respect the rules, yet each society operates in their fashion."

I was genuinely interested in the ways of my society.

"Time is the most important asset a human has. The only way we buy time is by disciplining ourselves and learning things faster than others would normally do. The society prides itself on its rigorous time management system."

Liam and I listened as the trainer lectured us.

"You will have a little over an hour to memorize not only the countries, but also the cities, the population, and the addresses of all the businesses we have spread across North, Central, and South America."

After giving us specific instructions, Liam and I did not waste time memorizing everything we had to learn. At the time, I thought memorizing something as detailed as that was, ironically, a waste of time. Either way, I had no choice but to study the countries and the locations of the other societies. The most important part was to do it effectively. I tried to see if there was a pattern between all the locations, but there was not. There was no option but to learn all the countries along with all the cities in business. After one hour, the trainer walked in to test us on our memory skills.

"All right, gentlemen, time is up. It is now time for the test."

The trainer handed us a blank sheet with the map of

the Americas.

It was now time to demonstrate everything I had been able to grasp in a short period of time. It was odd, but Liam and I finished around the same time. I had turned in the paper, knowing there were two locations I had missed. The room was silent while the trainer checked both of our papers.

"Well, gentlemen, I must say that I am quite impressed with the work you have done. Both of you were able to label a significant number of locations in a short amount of time. You have earned twenty-five minutes of spare time."

We both walked out of the room happy to have passed the test. After our break, we went back to the room to take applied mathematics, which would be useful for the real world.

Once our lesson was finished, we gathered at the dinner table, where the trainer had prepared a nice meal.

I don't know why, but Liam trusted me from the very beginning. Every night we would speak of the things we used to do back when we were not in training. Unlike me, Liam had a large family. However, he was the only boy because his brother had passed away when he was very young. Our conversations would go on until it was time for us to go to sleep.

One week had passed, and the focus of the training was mostly the same. We began every morning with the obstacle course that I had not yet gotten used to. It got me winded every time, but I was beginning to make fewer errors. Liam, like always, would complete the task with great ease. This particular session lasted around two hours. The trainer gave us a few minutes before commencing our usual geographical studies.

Liam and I went straight into the back room where we would usually take our classes. On this particular day, we did something different. The trainer talked about scuba diving. He explained everything, from the equipment to how to equalize the pressure underwater. For some reason, I was so invested in soaking in everything I could about scuba diving. The trainer had written down everything he had said on a whiteboard with wheels. He left Liam and me all alone so that we could study. We both found the information fascinating, which made it easy for us to grasp all the knowledge that was transmitted to us by our trainer.

The trainer came back to the room an hour later to test our knowledge. We completed the test in under half an hour. The trainer was thrilled to know that none of us had gotten any questions wrong.

For the rest of the week, we learned about the ocean and were tested regularly on the subject, with good scores.

After a month, anyone would have gotten accustomed to the groove of things. Each morning, I woke up a bit before the air horn so I could get a proper stretch in. The obstacle course was still the same, most likely because the trainer wanted us to get used to the routine of daily exercise. During this month, we learned about the different investments the Canadian Society had spread across five continents. It is safe to say that our geographical knowledge has expanded during that period, and I am delighted, as I have a keen interest in cultures from all over the world.

The following day, our trainer prepared something different. After we had gotten our short break, Liam and I headed towards the cabin, where the trainer awaited us.

"Alright. Today we will be doing something different," he announced. "For the last month we have been learning all about scuba diving, and today we will actually get to do it."

I was unsure what Liam was feeling currently, but I was certainly excited.

"You will find everything you need for our next session in the cabin. And please don't take too long."

The trainer finished the sentence before leaving our side.

We stepped inside the cabin, where all the equipment we required was placed on the dining table. Both the wetsuits were the same color but in different sizes. We put on our wetsuits, along with our weight belts.

It did not take us too long to stand in front of the trainer again. The trainer stood just a few feet away from the pool area. Before diving, the trainer gave us an overview of how to equalize our pressure. Both Liam and I jumped simultaneously in the pool after the trainer was done giving instructions. All we had to do was freely swim underwater, but we had to do it the right way because I knew the trainer was outside looking at us. I was enjoying myself so much that I did not want to leave the pool.

The sound of a high-pitched whistle made Liam and me exit from the water.

"Great job. Take the equipment back to the cabin."

It was one hour past noon, marking the customary lunchtime. While the dietary habits of the participants were secondary to the acquisition of knowledge and physical training, maintaining a low body fat percentage remained essential. The trainer emphasized that selecting appropriate foods and preparing nutritious meals was a worthwhile investment of our time. Consequently, we dedicated approximately an hour to preparing a tomato soup accompanied by a healthy salad. Upon completion, the trainer received a small portion of the salad, while Liam generously distributed equal portions of the soup and salad to each of us.

We maintained the same routine for the following two weeks: wake up, do the obstacle course, and study something different each day, along with strengthening our diving skills.

It all changed one particular day when the trainer told us to take our diving equipment to the car and wait patiently for him. I was both thrilled and somewhat worried as to what we were actually going to do.

Even though the drive was long, it was nice because I

got to relax both mentally and physically.

We arrived at a small dock, where the trainer directed us to a small boat, which was in poor condition. Liam and I jumped in before the trainer. I looked around because the place was beautiful. The trainer removed the rope from the cleat and sailed away into open waters.

After a significant amount of time, the trainer stopped at a spot where the tide was not that high. From the outside, I kept a confident body language. However, it was the first time that I was going to dive into the cold, gloomy ocean, which worried me. The trainer waited for Liam and me to put on our wetsuits.

"You must find your flags within the one-hour mark. If you don't, you will be swimming back to the dock." The trainer said once we had finished putting all our equipment on.

Anxiety started to hit me like never before.

"Do I make myself clear?" asked the trainer. We nodded. I stood there like a statue while Liam dove into the ice-cold water. I decided to clear my mind and do the same thing Liam did.

Immersing myself in the water felt different. At first, I was a bit nervous, but that all went away after telling myself that everything was going to be fine. Slowly, I started to descend into the much deeper and colder part of the ocean. A row of fish passed by me. Despite my bright headlight, I struggled to see underwater. Plenty of time had passed, and I had not managed to capture the flag. More and more fish kept swimming around me. It was irritating that I had not yet found the flag that I was looking for. After vigorously searching, I was able to locate it, floating inside a transparent box that was lit by a neon blue light. This technology was used by our society to search for things that were hidden in the ocean by other members using similar technologies. The downside is that it only worked at certain depths.

At last, I exited the gloomy water. However, there was a slight problem, which was the fact that I found myself all alone. This made me furious; it meant that I had to swim all the way back. The journey back was long and desolate. I didn't even know if I was heading in the right direction. I was exhausted and needed to take a breather. Behind me, I heard the engine of a boat, but I wondered if it was just my brain playing tricks with me. It wasn't; it was none other than the trainer, along with Liam.

"Need a lift?" the trainer asked.

The joke came at a time when I was not in the mood to speak to my trainer. Liam offered his hand, which I accepted.

I didn't think I would get on the boat. Liam was kind enough to hand me over a towel, which I used to warm my body up. We made it to our destination. Liam got off first. I followed him shortly after. My hands were heavy from swimming and carrying the scuba tank. As soon as

I reached the car, I put all of my gear in the trunk. It was not long before the trainer came and drove us back to the cabin.

Back at home we had a light lunch; this was a good moment, perhaps, for all of us. The trainer had instructed us to wait for him outside the cabin, near one of the trees. We calmly waited, even though I was eager to know what was going on.

"What are we going to do now?"

He looked at me and replied, "Meditate."

The trainer stepped out shortly after.

"Alright, Charles, this is the time when we relax our minds, so please, close your eyes and clear your head."

I followed his instructions and did what I was told. Being in a high-pressure situation, I entered a state of meditation for around fifteen minutes. I shut everything off, only hearing the beautiful sounds of nature.

"Alright, we're done," said the trainer. I opened my eyes and felt as good as new. I looked at Liam, who was in a relaxed state as well. "Let's go back inside."

After the meditation session, we took an hour break before heading to our evening cardio session. Cardio was not particularly hard; however, doing it at the end of the day made it unbearably challenging.

The following three weeks we didn't do anything out of the routine, like diving in open waters. Instead, we began to learn all about computer systems. I found this particular subject quite interesting. The professor would test us on different areas throughout the week. While I passed the exams with great ease, Liam struggled to understand some concepts. Nonetheless, with a bit of my help, he ended up passing all his exams comfortably. Once we completed the exams, Liam would not stop thanking me for my help.

Three months later, I was finally comfortable doing the training course. Just when I had started getting the hang of it, the trainer began adding more obstacles. The trainer clearly explained to us the importance of daily improvement. Since I had already gotten used to the intense training course, the trainer felt there was no need for us to get a break.

It was now time for the trainer to introduce to us a few martial arts.

"Alright, gentlemen, this exercise is a bit simpler compared to the other exercise. But you will need to pay attention if you are to learn proper self-defense techniques."

Since it was my first time doing martial arts, I couldn't do the proper technique. That is, until the trainer demonstrated the exercise himself. We started with the basics of form. Both of us kept messing up and not doing it the way the trainer wanted it to be. An hour passed, and our arms were tired. The trainer demanded more from us. He kept saying the enemy was strong and powerful, that we would need to train hard if we wanted to defeat him.

The trainer showed some sympathy, letting us have a

breather before our last exercise. I found it odd that Liam was as tired as I was. Standing in the middle, being authoritative as always, he said.

"I want one hundred push-ups, one hundred jumping jacks, and one hundred sit-ups."

There was no arguing against the word of the trainer, just the determination to end the day on the right note. Liam waited for me to tackle the task at the same time. Pushing through the pain was tough, I will admit. However, we both successfully managed to finish the task.

"Take a shower and get some rest," the trainer said, finally finishing our lesson.

"Wait for me here; I will bring you a fresh set of clothes," Liam added.

I nodded in approval. With no remaining energy left, I looked up to the stars, lying on my back. It was quite a sight until the trainer approached me and said-

"Good work today; start getting used to it. More complicated tasks await us."

He left quickly, not giving me the chance to reply. Liam returned with a set of clothes for each of us. The shower was pleasant, which helped cool down our bodies after the strenuous exercise.

Laying down in my cozy tent, many thoughts came to my mind. What is all this about? It has been an experience, to say the least. I went to bed with no energy left for anything else.

After our daily obstacle course training, we went to the back room, where the trainer was already waiting at his large wooden desk. He had placed an old, boxed TV in front of the two tables where we would normally attend our classes. It was the first time that the trainer had brought a TV, which caught my attention.

"Before we begin, I need to tell you that life is all about comprehension. The line between a life-and-death situation can be as simple as comprehension."

He got up from his chair and inserted a VHS tape kept inside a white box. Then he turned off the light. The documentary started in the Egyptian era and forwarded all the way to the present day; it was one of the most interesting things I had ever seen. The documentary offered a thorough explanation of how the environment, culture, and times influence a person's behavior. What I found most interesting was learning the different types of ways people might react to certain moments. Once the documentary ended after almost two hours, the trainer turned on the lights.

"I will not be testing you today; I will only ask, what do you think was the most important part of the video?"

I didn't understand, and from the looks of it, Liam didn't know what to say either.

"There is no right or wrong answer, boys; share your thoughts."

"The most important lesson I learned from the film

is to observe every detail around you. We react based on what we see and know."

I decided to take the initiative because Liam was not answering anytime soon.

"What about you, Liam? What are your thoughts?" the trainer went on to ask Liam.

"I believe Charles has summarized it perfectly."

The trainer nodded before dismissing us.

It was time for lunch, rice and salmon, which tasted delicious. Liam and I took our time; after around forty-five minutes, we had fully finished our meals. The trainer was nowhere to be found, but since we couldn't leave without his permission, Liam decided to pull out a chessboard from the closet.

"I've never played chess." I told him.

He looked at me. "Don't worry, I will quickly teach you how to play."

For approximately twenty minutes, he provided me with specific instructions on how to play the game. We started a game, and I went first because I was playing white. I made a random move. Liam analyzed my move, and then he moved quickly. It didn't take him long to start taking my pieces and gaining control of the game. This wasn't a game that I was familiar with, so I didn't care if I won or lost. Finally, he put me in checkmate. After my defeat, we would go on to discuss the different plays that chess players utilized. Our conversation would last until the trainer came to where we were.

"Alright boys, get ready for craft work."

We walked out after cleaning up the mess we had left in the trainer's home. At last, it was finished. The trainer stood outside waiting for us. He reminded us about the importance of using our surroundings. He filled us up with valuable information. Our next task sounded simpler than it was: we were required to create a weapon using our surroundings in under two hours.

Being in the forest was both an advantage and a disadvantage. The lack of time and my urgency led me to build the most obvious weapon possible: a bow and an arrow. Apart from protecting you, they were also a handy tool to catch some food.

The initial task at hand was crafting the bow. I assessed the surrounding area to identify the types of trees available. My knowledge of tree species was limited, but I soon realized that I required a material that was both strong and flexible, yet light and maneuverable. The majority of trees in the forest were pine, which I deemed unsuitable due to their relatively thin and soft characteristics. Eventually, I located a suitable maple tree. I carefully carved various sections of the trunk, although my technique was relatively unrefined at this stage. The most challenging aspect was shaping the bow itself to ensure its functionality, a process that took approximately thirty minutes. Subsequently, I added the characteristic slight curve that most bows possess, and the final step involved cutting notches necessary for affixing the strings.

At this point, the job was halfway finished. It was now time to move on to the arrow. I set off again to find a useful tree. I did not need the thickest of trees; a small pine tree would help me. Carving it was a difficult process because I had to make it as straight as I could. After making a perfectly straight stick, I had to focus on the point. In the limited amount of time that I had, I made the arrowhead as sharp as I could.

My biggest test awaited me. In search of a string for my bow, I had no idea where to begin. With my bow in hand, I went directly to my tent, hoping to find something useful, although there was not much that could help. I needed to find something elastic enough to be used as a string. After searching restlessly, I managed to find a plant that, I thought, could be useful. I removed the part I needed before tying the fibers together in a clockwork motion. Once the strings were finished, I applied the strings directly towards the notch of the bow.

After completing the stringing process, I pulled one of the arrows on the string, just to make sure that it worked properly. My inexperience caused me to miss my target. However, the fact that the arrow did work was indeed great news.

I headed back to the cabin, where the trainer was already waiting for me.

"What do we have here?" the trainer asked.

"A bow and an arrow, sir."

The trainer gently took my weapon from my hands. I stood in the back, watching as he examined my weapon. The trainer did not hide any expression; instead, he took a random shot into a tree, which he landed.

"Not bad, but could have been better," said the trainer.

He walked back to where Liam was standing. I was so focused on my objective that I had not noticed what Liam had built. The initial item was a wooden shield, which I found intriguing. However, what fascinated me was the double-edged spear. Liam was very intelligent when it came to building weapons. He not only knew that he had to protect himself from arrows but also that he needed a weapon for close-range combat. The trainer knocked on the wood of the shield to see if it was strong enough. He also picked up the spear and began to swing freely before heading it back to Liam.

"Good work, Liam," were his words.

I picked up the bow and arrow before walking back. Liam and I walked together, as usual.

"I thought your weapon was better than mine," he said.

"No way, yours was significantly better than mine," I replied, looking back at him.

Liam went inside his tent to get some rest. I, on the

other hand, was not tired enough, so I did something that would relax me even more. I grabbed my bow and arrow, hoping to practice my archery skills.

While searching for an appropriate practice location, I encountered an intriguing waterfall and decided to assess the water temperature by touching it. As anticipated, it was refreshingly cold. The soothing sounds of the waterfall compelled me to take a brief dip. While in the water, I noticed a series of interconnected tubes, the purpose of which I could not immediately ascertain. I positioned myself beneath the cascade, allowing the water to cascade directly onto me. Aware that my trainer might call for me at any moment, I only lingered for a short while. After a few minutes, I emerged from the water, dressed, and retrieved my bow. Despite my intention to leave, I found it difficult to resist examining the tubes further. Following their path, I discovered it led to the training course, where the pool was located. This observation led me to conclude that the pool was fed by the stream. I returned to the cascade to enjoy a few more moments in its refreshing embrace.

The whole experience had been full of surprises. The following week would not be much different. It was about six o'clock, and the sun was beginning to set. Liam and I thought the day was over, but the trainer had a different plan.

"A few weeks ago, you learned how to use your surroundings to build a weapon. Today, you will learn how to use the weapons that have already been established. Pick your weapons quickly and head towards the car."

Both of us walked towards the inside of the cabin, where there were various handguns on the couch and multiple rifles on the living room table. Liam and I were impressed by the abundance of firearms. Since my experience with weapons was minimal, I picked the lightest handguns. Before we left, the trainer told me to take a rifle with a scope. I went back to pick the best available option.

After a somewhat short car drive, we found ourselves at a deserted gun range. Outside, there were numerous mannequins set up as a hitting range. The trainer had gone through the specifics of how a gun works and what we needed to do before beginning the exercise. He displayed his mastery, hitting the furthest target on the head several times without missing a shot. Liam's turn was up. He was using one of the sniper rifles he had picked up back home. It took him a while to set it up, and given the great focus needed to hit the target, he completely missed the first shot.

"Take your time and focus."

Liam paused and took a deep breath. This was the first time I had seen Liam getting nervous. The noise was loud, disturbing the peace on the deserted gun range. He was more accurate this time, managing to hit the mannequin's waist. Utilizing his binoculars, the trainer analyzed the shot.

"Great job, you have done significant damage to your enemy."

We were there for a while, until Liam had no more shots left. Every attempt was better than his last, making it really tough for me to beat.

"Wait here," said the trainer.

I congratulated Liam for his amazing work while the trainer was setting up another mannequin. Liam gave me the confidence I needed, as he kept encouraging me. It was my turn. I positioned myself nicely behind the sniper rifle. I measured the distance from where I was to the mannequin, which was further than I had anticipated. A few minutes later, I still was not sure about the exact distance. I inhaled briefly before firing my gun.

"Hold," said the trainer.

I was looking through the scope to determine if I had hit the right spot.

"Great work," said the trainer. I finished the session on an excellent note.

Even if it was our first day, we did not fare as badly as we expected. Going to the deserted shooting range would become part of our daily task. Each day, Liam and I improved our accuracy and our composure.

My fear was tested on a random day when the trainer drove us to a small private airport. We got out of the car and followed him, who still hadn't told us what we were doing there. He led us to a small indoor office where a man in his forties was standing, completely focused on his computer monitor.

The trainer and the man exchanged hugs when they saw each other.

"What do we have here?" asked the man while staring at us."

The trainer looked at him before answering.

"These boys need the usual training."

The man looked at us one more time before turning towards the trainer.

"Are you sure?"

The trainer answered with a simple nod.

The trainer left us with the man, who was hesitant at first. It took him some time, but he eventually came to terms with his duty. He took us to the back and showed us all the basics of skydiving. Even though the thought of skydiving on your own can be a bit terrifying, it was quite the opposite for me.

After around an hour, the man had finally finished his explanation, and it was time for us to pick the wingsuit of our choice. I picked the red and white one, while Liam picked the yellow and blue. After this, the man led us to the back of the airport, where a mid-sized airplane was waiting for us. Two men were sitting on a pair of chairs, smoking cigars. The skydiving instructor interrupted them.

"We have two young men who wish to skydive."

They exchanged looks of disbelief.

The gentleman stated in a serious tone, "It is not my call." Still, they were a bit skeptical.

This all ended when our instructor said, "If you guys don't fly that airplane, then we will all lose our jobs."

One of them threw his cigar on the floor, putting it out with his foot, and went to the plane to perform a quick inspection. The other man remained reluctant in his seat until eventually deciding to help his partner. The skydiving instructor told us to be calm and to remember to release our parachutes at approximately five thousand feet. He wished us well before he left. Liam and I stood there for around half an hour waiting for the pilots to do their job.

Finally, the pilots had finished, and we were ready to go. The loud noise of the airplane's engine didn't help relieve the butterflies I felt in my stomach. Slowly, the airplane took off. I was by the window, trying my best to calm myself down. The views of my country were absolutely stunning. At a fair pace, the airplane was slowly ascending. I refused to get nervous. One of the pilots opened the door and shouted over the noise, "Good luck, boys."

Suddenly, a refreshing breeze filled the cabin as we prepared for our jump. Liam exchanged a glance with me and confidently took the lead, leaping out of the airplane without hesitation. Although I did not look back, I understood it was now my turn. Summoning every ounce of courage, I followed suit and exited the aircraft. Strangely, I felt no fear as I floated through the air, acutely aware of our insignificance amidst the vastness of this beautiful planet. I attempted to locate Liam but, not seeing him, felt reassured in the knowledge that he was safe. As I embraced the experience, I began to engage in various maneuvers in the air, which alleviated any lingering doubts I had. Before I knew it, it was almost time to deploy my parachute. Uncertain, I opted to wait before making that critical decision.

I found myself gradually nearing the ground. My instinct told me to release the parachute before it was too late. Luckily, I had no problem with it; my only issue was not knowing where I was going to land. I looked down to check where I was heading, but I had no clue. It seemed like I was going to land on a farm field, which, I believed, was the perfect landing spot.

Eventually, I landed there without any trouble whatsoever. Initially, I had difficulty removing my parachute, but after some time, I remembered what the instructor had said and was able to figure it out. I stood up and found myself in a location I had never been to before. I walked for miles, trying to get a notion as to where I was. The area was pretty deserted, as was the road. For many hours, I sat on the ground, but not a single car passed by. The sun was beginning to set, and I was running out of options. My decision was not the best, but it was the only one that I could make: walk back and try to see if there was somebody by the farmhouse. The farm was full of cows and sheep. The house was a different story, however. For many minutes, I circled the house, trying to find someone who could help. Several times I knocked on the door, but no one would answer. It was getting annoying, so I decided to open the door myself.

The house was small and abandoned. The floors would make an irritating noise, making it awfully terrifying. In addition, the house was decorated with creepy farm toys, which worsened the energy of the place. Either way, it was not my concern; my focus was directed towards finding someone who could hold. I proceeded to enter the room, which was empty except for a pedestal fan. Seconds later, I entered the second room, where I would encounter a dead body. This was the moment when I wanted to run out of that place, but for some strange reason, I didn't. Out of nowhere, police cars arrived at the home. I decided not to do anything; it would look suspicious. Police officers broke the door without knocking and sprinted into the room where I was. They shouted, Freeze! And immediately, I put my hands up without saying a word.

I was alone inside a small interrogation room at the police station, calmly waiting for the detective to ask me a few questions. I was bored and thirsty at the same time. An old man with a good physique stepped inside the room and sat in front of me.

"What were you doing at the farmhouse?"

I was extremely reluctant to answer, thinking he wouldn't believe me. I did not have many options but to give him a clear answer about what had happened.

"May I have a glass of water?" The man immediately made a signal to the window.

"I was skydiving and landed at the farm. I walked towards the road, where I stood for a few hours." Another officer came in and placed the water in front of me. I stopped telling him the story to get a nice sip of water.

"You were skydiving by yourself?"

It was difficult to even look at him with a straight face.

"Yes." I replied with a confident tone.

The meeting was interrupted by the same man who had brought the water to me, telling the detective that he had a message for him. He left the room while I sat patiently wondering when I could leave. It took him a while, but the main detective finally came back to the room with the news: I was free to go. The detective led me to the main desk of the police station, where my trainer and Liam were awaiting me. Both of them asked me if I was alright, and I answered with a simple nod.

"I hope this will not happen again," the trainer told the detective in a very imposing manner.

The years passed, and, slowly, I got better at every single aspect of my training. Liam had already finished his training, and I hadn't heard anything about him ever since. On the second to last day, I had to take the ultimate test, which was an examination of both my mental and physical state.

The trainer took me back to somewhere familiar; it was the house where I had accepted the training. I was told this would be like my graduation, so I wore a beautiful gray suit with a blue tie. Inside the house, many men were gathered, dressed in an expensive suit, similar to the one I was wearing. The men began to clap the minute I stepped foot in the door. A middle-aged man wearing a red tie led me to the conference room.

It was a large and spacious room, where the Canadian leader was sitting at the head of a table. He stood up when I entered the room and congratulated me by offering his hand. He gave me my diploma, which I had definitely earned. Subsequently, he placed a medal around my neck. After all the praise I got for him, he asked me to step outside; someone special was waiting for me.

Something shocking happened when I stepped outside. I saw my father, who was also dressed for the occasion, like the rest of us. It was quite the moment for us; we had not seen each other for six years.

"Charles, you look great!"

"As do you," I told my father.

We exchanged hugs before entering the mansion.

CHAPTER 3

THE LAST LIGHT

Birkir was proud that I successfully completed his training with commendable scores. Reuniting with my father after six long years was an indescribable feeling. Initially, I was uncertain about accepting the training he proposed, but as time went on, I realized that my decision was the best one I could have made. It provided me with invaluable experiences and knowledge that most civilians would only wish to acquire. Two thoughts predominated in my mind: what would happen next, and how my mother would react upon seeing me for the first time.

After I met with my father, the leader of the Canadian society invited me over to the house where he had prepared a dinner with most of the members of the Canadian society. The members and I spent quality time with each other; we, of course, spoke about everything except society-related matters.

As we were enjoying our meal, which was quite splendid, a special guest walked towards the dining room to occupy one of the free seats. That guest was none other than Birkir, who was appreciated by the members of the society and especially popular with the young members such as myself.

The conversation around the long, circular table continued for a considerable duration. Once the members had finished their meals and were preparing to enjoy dessert, expertly prepared by the talented culinary staff, the Canadian leader—seated at the head of the table—stood to gently tap his glass of rosé wine. Shortly thereafter, the lively discussions subsided, and the room's attention was promptly directed toward the society's leader.

"Pardon my interruption, gentlemen, but there is one thing I would like to say." The respect the members had for the leader was highlighted at this precise moment, where you could see the deep commitment that every member had for our leader.

"As we know, nothing in life is easy. Difficulty arises in every aspect of our lives. Challenges are not only faced within our responsibility; they are also faced outside our roles as members. As you know, many people try to become one of us. Each individual has their distinctive motives, but not everyone has what it takes to carry the weight of our roles. " During this speech, I made a strange reflection, which was the fact that none of the staff members would come near us while the leader was delivering his powerful speech.

"Today, however, is not the day for negative reflections or to think about what could have happened. That is not why we are gathered. We are here to celebrate the efforts of two men. One who has shaped both the present and the past of this society and another who will potentially shape our future. " The leader of Canada was referring to Birkir and me. My father, who was proudly sitting next to me, gave me a nice pat on the back, acknowledging my accomplishments.

"I would like to raise my glass to congratulate these men and to wish a prosperous future for our country and our society."

All the proud members in the room did not hesitate to raise a glass for the future of the society.

"Please enjoy desserts, gentlemen, if you will excuse me. I have some business to attend to." The leader said, while leaving the members at the table.

The friendly house staff came with a small menu, which had several dessert options. Usually members don't eat many sweets, but occasionally, it is important that we do consume a specific amount of sugar to protect our bodies. On the menu there were various tasty options for selection, but for some reason I was desiring a plain caramel ice cream, something I had not eaten in a long time. My father, on the other hand, ordered a plain yogurt, which is something I found interesting. His choice was influenced by the fact that he was much older, and as you age, you need to take care of your body more.

The table was less filled than when I arrived, since not all members were particularly interested in having dessert. Fortunately for the members who decided to remain, the staff returned fairly quickly with our desserts. My strawberry ice cream had a minimalistic decoration, which I did not mind. Without hesitation, I tried the ice cream, which had an incredibly rich flavor that delighted my taste buds.

"It's good, isn't it?" My father asked, while I simply nodded my head.

"Don't worry, I gave them the recipe." My father said in a lighthearted manner.

As I was enjoying my ice cream, I couldn't help but notice that Birkir was no longer present. At the time, I had not been paying close attention to his whereabouts, but I felt a sense of disappointment upon realizing that he was no longer with us.

Even though I believed Birkir was no longer at the establishment, I was incorrect about my assumption. Birkir was actually busy having a private meeting with the leader of Canada in his office.

"Quite the speech." Birkir who was standing by the

door of his office, said.

"It is only necessary; both you and Charles deserve it." The leader said, while pouring himself a small cup of espresso coffee he had made from his high-end coffee machine.

"Please have a seat." The Canadian leader kindly requested Birkir.

"I was hoping this would not take too long."

"Time is a complicated thing, and certain topics need to be discussed with more depth." Despite Birkir's reluctant attitude, he opted to take a seat in front of the leader himself.

The leader of the Canadian society would walk towards the table to take a seat and hand Birkir a nice cup of warm coffee.

"Thanks but I've had enough for today." Birkir politely declined.

"As you wish, but I must say, you are truly missing out." The leader replied while Birkir simply chuckled.

"I know it is not the custom, but talk to me about your recent student." The leader said after taking a small sip of his coffee.

"Did you read the reports?" Birkir asked.

"Oh yes, the results were astonishing." The Canadian leader replied with a sense of pride he usually does not demonstrate with other students.

"He is the best student I ever had." Birkir said, in a

very confident manner.

"I know, his results are among the best in any society's history." The Canadian leader would go on to take yet one more sip of his coffee, while Birkir would simply stare at him.

"All credit to his trainer, of course." The leader told Birkir, intending to give him some words of encouragement.

"As you know, I have trained many boys over the years; some have been more qualified than others, but the results Charles has shown are something I had not previously witnessed." The leader of the Canadian Society would simply nod his head, agreeing with the words of Birkir.

"Politely I would like to ask, what do you want from me?" Birkir asked, simply wanting to finish the night.

"Well, for starters, I would want you to reconsider your retirement."

"Not an option. I want to take care of my health and my personal family." Birkir, he said, confident of his decision.

"Who wouldn't want to."

"Well, while I can't convince you, I would like to kindly ask for a favor from you." This statement from the leader was made while he leaned slightly forward to better address his situation.

"As you know, the Conference of Nations is just around the corner. Several topics will be discussed, including the rise of a collective group made up of mainly northern European nations that were part of the old Soviet Union."

"I know a thing or two about that." Birkir replied, referring to the Soviet Union, although he was unaware of the new group.

"This new group is called the NEU; they are looking to bring unconventional changes to our society. It is essential that we know what is going on." Birkir remained calm, but he did have a contemplative attitude.

"Why do you want me to go?" Birkir curiously asked.

"You are my most loyal man. Besides, we are the only ones who understand how northern Europeans work."

"While I am afraid, I can't fulfill your wishes. I know someone that could help."

"What a pity." The Canadian leader replied.

"You won't be disappointed; Liam is loyal and a good listener." Birkir replied, while the Canadian leader simply nodded his head.

"Has our meeting ended?. Sir." The leader looked at him with a slight smile, all while simultaneously nodding his head.

The Conference of Nations, held biennially and hosted in different locations, is designed to ensure the safety of our members by creating ambiguity for outsiders who might seek to disrupt our society. This year, the conference will be held in the stunning city of Moscow. Although the leader's intentions are not entirely transparent, I believe that his close relationship with Birkir, combined with his experience working within what was formerly known as the Soviet Union, influenced his decision to send Birkir to this event.

This conference is regarded with great seriousness, as it serves as an important forum for members to convene with representatives from other nations to discuss various issues of mutual concern. It also provides an opportunity for nations to establish new societal policies. For members of our society, the conference is viewed as a valuable occasion to foster better understanding and strengthen international relationships. While the event is typically hosted in different venues each year, there are instances when it is held within the same country.

Each country observes its own traditions before the commencement of the conference. As Russia was the host nation this year, they chose to organize a theatrical performance accompanied by an orchestra.

Birkir's decision to abstain from attending the conference was not due to a lack of willingness to represent his country, but rather because he believed that someone younger should represent our society. He felt a sense of responsibility in recommending a suitable candidate for this role. Given his experience, Birkir was confident that Liam was well-qualified to serve in this capacity.

Liam is an intelligent and highly accessible individual. His readiness to support others is a key aspect of his demeanor. Liam's success stems not only from his personal achievements but also from his adeptness at guiding others toward their best selves. He conveyed a personal philosophy during a training session, emphasizing that positive collaboration is essential for individual progress and can significantly shape one's outlook.

While I was still training, Liam was doing different tasks that I was not aware of due to the confidentiality of his objectives. When Liam received the call from his old trainer, he was proud to learn that his trainer had chosen him for such an important task.

Liam accepted his role, having permission from the Canadian leader to halt his current duty to attend the conference of nations. At the time of the news, Liam was not specifically in Canada, although it wasn't an issue for the society to get a private plane that would take him directly to Moscow.

Liam's journey to Moscow was relatively smooth, but he was nonetheless troubled by a lingering concern: the fact that the meeting was scheduled to take place in a single day. He questioned whether he was adequately prepared for the potential outcomes that might arise. Despite this apprehension, he understood the importance of remaining composed, recognizing that he needed to absorb all the necessary information.

The landing of his plane was smooth, which is always something to be thankful for. During the call with Birkir, Liam expressed the desire not to be driven to his destination. Society members are usually allowed to have drivers in foreign countries, but as a general recommendation, we never tell the driver the exact location we are staying at. This is to protect what we consider to be the most important thing to us, our discretion. Having someone you are not particularly familiar with know where you are staying is not always the best thing.

Since Liam was a new member, he had not generated enough wealth or status for the society to rent him a high-end car. Birkir had chosen a Toyota RAV4, a car that is not very flamboyant but does the job. Liam was simply happy to have a ride of his own and not have someone else drive him. Without a pinch of hesitation, Liam accommodated his things in the back part of the trunk before finally departing from the airport.

In the midst of all the pressure, Liam was happy to be in Moscow. Like many members of our society, Liam genuinely enjoyed visiting other countries. Russia, in particular, was a place that caught his attention. The complicated history of Russia, along with the numerous amount of interesting people the country has been able to produce, was something that he found fascinating. Liam believed that the people of Russia might seem cold and unwelcoming to foreign individuals, but from his standpoint, they were fierce people who endured brutal wars, as well as radical political situations, that shaped their current attitude towards life.

As he kept driving through the busy city, he could not help but admire the natural beauty of the country. He was fortunate enough to come across modern and old buildings while heading towards his temporary residence.

Liam arrived in the city of Moscow at approximately three thirty, meaning the traffic was not too busy, although, as time passed, it was commencing to get slightly busier.

Moscow is a large and complex city, where you could easily get lost while driving. Fortunately for Liam, he reviewed the address of his residence multiple times before the plane landed in the city. It did not take Liam long to arrive at the parking lot of the residence that he would be calling home for the next few days.

Since the society had strict security measures, the apartment complex that Liam would reside in happened to be in a wealthy area, which was protected by the police. The man in the hut was tall and overweight and had a long black beard. At that moment, the man was not very familiar with Liam; therefore, his treatment towards him was significantly cold. Liam did not mind; instead, he complied with the man, who had asked him if he was a visitor or a resident. Liam replied by saying that he was a visitor but that he had rented a room in the establishment. The man asked him for his identification before going inside the hut to check if he was indeed telling him the truth.

It would not take long for the man to verify all the information and determine that Liam was being honest. The man returned to him with his identification, as well as a document he had to show to the person that would await him at the reception. Liam simply thanked him before finding a parking spot.

The parking garage was relatively busy, which posed a minor inconvenience for Liam, as he had to park on the upper levels, farther from the exit. Nonetheless, he proceeded to the top floor, searching for a parking space. Without hesitation, Liam turned off the engine and quickly gathered his belongings, determined to minimize any delay.

Even though the temperatures outside were cold, the temperature inside the garage was warm, thanks to the heating system the garage had installed. Liam would encounter a slight issue, which was that it took some time to find the elevator that would lead him towards the reception. This occurred because the instructions on the garage were mainly in Russian, and Liam wasn't proficient enough with the language to fully understand his direction. Nonetheless, he was able to find the elevator after a few minutes.

Liam entered the elevator, which was modern and beautiful. The inside was clean and empty, which was a bonus for Liam, who did not want to run into other residents, not because he was unfriendly, but to keep a low profile in the middle of a critical moment. The elevator would descend to the first floor, where it would lead him to the stunning lobby of the apartment.

This time it would not take Liam long to locate the reception, where a young Russian lady worked on her computer.

"Izvinite, vy govorite po-angliyski?" Liam politely asked the Russian lady if she spoke English.

"Yes, I do. How may I help?" the young lady replied.

"I have booked a room for a couple of days." Liam said.

"You are Peter, am I right?" The lady asked Liam for his incognito name, a name used by members to protect our true identity.

"Yes. I am indeed." Liam gladly replied.

"Perfect." The lady said, while reaching for the keys to his room.

"Here you are; your room is located on the third floor. If you prefer, I could upgrade you to a room on the upper floors, which offers a more expansive view of the city." The lady, who was fully committed to helping Liam, gave him the option of a complimentary upgrade.

"Thanks, but I like the number three." Liam gave her this silly response since the room was strategically selected by Birkir because of its proximity to the first floor.

"No problem, enjoy your stay. If you encounter any issues. Please let me know."

It was now time for Birkir to unwind from the sudden news of his important task he had ahead of him. Since his room was situated on the third floor, it did not take him long to finally reach his destination. The halls of the floor were spacious, and the length from one side of the floor to the other was not lengthy at all. This was good news because it meant that the floor did not have many rooms, adding more privacy to Liam, who was keen on maintaining a low profile.

Liam entered the room, which had a welcoming smell of lemons. It did not take long for Liam to walk around the room to explore the different features it had. Although the apartment had everything a person would need, it was not spacious. Liam did not mind; however, he was simply complacent about being in a place he considered to be safe.

After conducting a brief inspection of the room, Liam proceeded to adjust his clothing in the closet. During this process, he discovered a mid-sized safe. Without hesitation, Liam entered the combination provided to him by Birkir before his arrival in the country. The safe opened automatically upon entering the correct code, revealing its contents.

Inside the safe was a small envelope, along with a pin with the Canadian flag. Curious as to what was inside the envelope, Liam did not hesitate to open it. The envelope contained a train card, along with a letter specifically for Liam. The letter stated:

Dear Liam,

I would like to extend my congratulations. Out of many members, you have been chosen to represent our society. We are all proud of your achievements, and we believe that you are suitable to represent us at this upcoming conference.

As you know, every conference is slightly different. The Russian society has arranged an orchestra for its members. On the next page, you will see a set of instructions telling you how to arrive at the theater where the show will be held.

Like always, I wish you good luck. Please represent us in the best way possible; our relationship with the other societies is vital for our future.

My Best Regards,
Your leader.

Liam proceeded to review the set of instructions, which provided him with detailed information about the complexities involved in reaching the theater. After carefully examining each step, Liam felt the need for a drink commonly enjoyed in Russia. He walked to the refrigerator and retrieved a carton of orange juice, which he poured into a polished glass. Before taking a moment to himself, Liam also pulled out a bottle of vodka, which he intended to blend with the orange juice.

It was now finally time for Liam to simply enjoy himself. Liam sat in the living room, which overlooked the balcony, which from his angle had somewhat of a view of the street he was situated on. Liam opted not to sit outside, since it was cold, and he did not want to be seen too much.

For a significant amount of time, Liam sat on the comfortable couch, simply enjoying the tranquility of the apartment. Since Liam had no rush, he decided to take his time to finish his drink.

Approximately one hour and thirty minutes had gone by. While Liam took for himself, he decided that it was important to head to the train station, where he would be getting the train to get to the theater.

Following a rapid shower, Liam changed to clothes you would usually wear in the wintertime. Liam had to decide whether he would take his car to head to the train station or if he was going to walk towards his intended destination. Since it was most likely around six, Liam believed that there was going to be a bit of traffic; therefore, it was better if he took the nearest underground station to see how, well, everything functioned. After reviewing the underground system on his phone, Liam finally left the apartment, ready to head to the station.

Liam used the same elevator to head out into the extreme temperatures of Russia. The night was beginning to fall, but Liam did not mind because as the sun was beginning to set, the beautiful hues that the sky would set over the Russian skyline were a memory he personally captured utilizing the camera of his phone.

Apart from the beautiful skies, something that would capture Liam's attention was that the streets were not particularly crowded; sure, there were a few pedestrians casually walking by, but it did not seem as populated as other major cities. Liam was not too sure about why this occurred, but he believed it was because of the efficient infrastructure of the city.

Given the relatively sparse pedestrian traffic, Liam surveyed the diverse array of restaurants visible along the thoroughfare. After navigating a few intersections and undertaking a twelve-minute walk, Liam successfully located the metro station.

The inside was busier than the actual streets but was impeccably clean. Liam did not waste time to locate a wall that displayed all the stations. Once Liam located his station, he went directly to a ticket booth where he would purchase a ticket that would take him to different stations around the city.

The next station would be arriving in approximately six minutes; therefore, Liam did not waste time, heading towards the electric staircase that would lead him towards his train. Something that Liam considered fascinating was the beautiful design that would make you think that you are in a Russian gallery.

In the short wait time, Liam's attention was captured by his surroundings. However, he could not fully enjoy everything because the train arrived quicker than what he initially expected.

Liam was one of the first ones inside the train, where he managed to find a seat easily. The train would make three stops before arriving at its destination. Liam exited the train, where he would head directly towards the electric stairs that would take him to the station's main entry. From there, Liam walked all the way towards the theater, where there was a crowd of people waiting in line, ready to enter the building.

As Liam was taking a closer look, a young man with a slight German accent approached him and said.

"You are not here for the play, are you."

"No, the crowd just caught my eye." Liam replied, believing that the man was one of the ticket sellers of the theater.

"Either that, or you have a conference you need to attend." It did not take long for Liam to realize that the person he was speaking to was a member of a distinct society.

"What gave it away?" Liam asked

"Many things, but your friend Birkir had advised me of your presence.

"Just in case you are wondering, the conference starts in the morning." Liam looked confused while the man made the statement.

"How come I wasn't informed?"

"From the looks of it, there was a change of plan, and that's why I am here." Liam had many questions in his mind, but he did not want to ask, since it would make him look indiscreet.

"Be up at five; the show starts at seven, and the conference starts at nine. Meet me at the train station nearest to your residence."

"See you there." The man said, before leaving Liam's side.

Since it was Liam's first time attending the conference, and he was a fairly new member, he was not as experienced and used to the ways of the society, even though he understood them fairly well. This learning experience would not faze him; instead, he headed back to the train station, which would eventually take him towards his residence.

Liam successfully arrived at his residence, where he would quickly drink a cup of water and pour some water on his face to clean himself up instead of taking a shower. Change into his sleeping attire, set his alarm, and head directly to sleep.

Liam chose to go to bed early to ensure he was properly rested and ready for the following morning.

Despite the day's challenges, Liam secured the necessary rest to face the tasks ahead. His alarm sounded at the designated time. Liam's morning routine was straightforward. Upon rising, he performed light stretches to promote circulation and mental clarity. He then proceeded to the refrigerator for a simple breakfast of Greek yogurt and a small bowl of cereal.

Liam would go on to wash his teeth, before putting on his proper winter attire. In no time, he was ready to tackle his challenging day. Until this point, there was no present danger, however, no one knows what can actually occur, Liam decided to take a weapon that members are allowed to carry to the conference, the weapon that was allowed was a simple taser, not to harm each other, but to protect themselves from possible danger, without caring a proper gun. Liam would go on to exit, his residence, to head to the station.

Since it was early in the morning, the weather was at it's peak when it came to how cold it actually was. Coming from Canada, we were very much used to this freezing weather, but for members from much warmer climates, they were definitely going to feel it in their bones. The streets were desolate, and there was barely any traffic, providing Liam a quick arrival in the train station.

Given that it was outside designated operating hours,

the station was officially closed. However, to his surprise, the station door was open, providing Liam direct access to the entrance. The premises appeared to be unoccupied; nonetheless, the electric escalators were operational, and the lighting was partially functional.

Either way, Liam went to the train stop, where the same man, who had informed him about the schedule change was waiting for him. The first thing the man would do while making eye contact with Liam was clap in a very slow manner.

"Just on time." The man said, while Liam did not react.

"My real name is Friedrich by the way, I'll be representing the Austrian society." The man introduced himself to Liam for the first time.

"I believe you already know who I am." Liam replied, knowing that Friedrich already knew his name.

"Not quite, but I will get to know you better." Friedrich said, intending to say that even though he had some information about him, he did not know him personally.

While the men were interacting, the engine of the train got louder, signifying that it was approaching their location.

"I believe that is our ride." Friedrich said.

Something was different this time, which was the fact that the train looked slightly different from the one that usually circulates in the station. Liam did not react, instead he let his intuitive nature take control, of the possibility of asking a foolish question. Judging from the exterior, this unique train did seem more modern than their usual train.

The doors open revealing a slightly busy cabin of well-dressed men.

"Don't worry, those men are members just like you and me." Friedrich told Liam, most likely judging from his confused facial expression.

Both men would go on to take a seat at the first table they were able to find. The inside was as modern as the exterior of the train, the only distinction was that the interior was a bit more luxurious.

The train ride would take longer than expected, yet none of the representative members of the society would complain. The private train offered, world-class services that included breakfast, Liam did not have a clue about this; therefore he had eaten breakfast at his residence, but despite having eaten, he ordered an orange juice.

During the unexpectedly long train ride, Liam and Friedrich took the opportunity to engage in conversation. Members are typically cautious when speaking with others—especially with men from different societies. Fortunately, their discussion remained focused solely on the conference and its distinctive structure. As someone new to the entire experience, Liam absorbed the information eagerly, like a sponge.

Just when you thought, nothing out of the usual

would occur, the train cabin, went on a downward slope, which caught Liam of guard. Causing him to immediately turn his head to the window, where all he would see was pitch black.

"They didn't tell you anything, did they?" Friedrich asked, surprised about the minimal information that was given to Liam

"Russians, don't like conventional meeting places, or events, they always innovate, to let others know, they are not behind when it comes to creative projects."

"Where are we heading to?" A confused Liam asked.

"The conference of course," Friedrich simply replied.

The train ride would continue on for another thirty minutes, before finally coming to a complete stop.

"I believe this our stop." Friedrich said, as all the men in the train rose from their seats to depart the wagon.

Since, Liam was inexperienced, he opted to follow Friedrich's lead. The station was similarly designed, like the previous stations Liam had been in. The only difference was that this station had all the countries flags, along with a symbol of that specific country, for example, the Spanish flag had a vibrant picture, of the fighting bull, while the French had a beautiful picture of the arc of triumph. All these welcoming symbols led Liam to believe that he was indeed in the right place.

There were two ways to get to the theater where the meeting was about to take place, one was to go through the usual electric staircase, and the second option was to use the elevator. At the time, Liam was not aware, but due to the importance of the Canadian society, and the fact that the Canadian leader did not have a speech, he wished to convey. The leader had reserved a seat on the upper levels.

The elevator doors opened to reveal the expansive corridors of the grand theater. Liam, captivated by the surrounding splendor, was so absorbed that he did not think to inquire whether his seats were reserved. Finally, the group arrived at the theater's opulent entrance, a testament to its rich architectural heritage. The façade was intricately detailed, and the interior featured gilded moldings, plush velvet curtains, and dazzling chandeliers, creating an atmosphere of historical grandeur and artistic excellence. This majestic venue, dedicated to classical performances, ballet, opera, and dramatic arts, exemplified Russia's deep-rooted tradition of theatrical mastery. It was a place where timeless elegance and artistic heritage converged, providing an ideal setting for the upcoming performance.

It took around twenty minutes for all the members to settle on their seats. Once all the members were settled, the lights dimmed, indicating the show was about to begin. Before the show commenced, there was a speech from the leader of the host nation.

"Good morning gentleman." The Leader of Russia, now, known as the leader of the NEU said, to the crowd, which gave a similar reply.

"Firstly, it is always a pleasure, to have you guys here. Today will not only be a day of business, but a day of change, innovation. This year's conference will be marked in the history book, as one that change the way of the society for good." The theater remained quiet as the leader of the NEU was delivering his speech.

"Before, we commence our business, there will be a show that embodies who we are as a nation, it is my pleasure to present, the last light."

The leader of the NEU would walk off the stage, before all the members began to applaud, excited about the beginning of the show.

In a matter of seconds, the beautiful red curtain rose revealing a beautiful orchestra with all the essential instruments, the show captured the audience's attention, due to the unique blend of elements. The story revolved around a pregnant woman in the second world war, as we know, the second world war hit hard on the Russian population, causing them to lose many civilians. The family of the woman who happened to be the protagonist of the show, slowly started passing away, making her the last person in her bloodline. It was an unfortunate situation, that this young lady had to endure. However, she met a soldier who she fell in love with. Despite, her not wanting him to return to the battlefield, the man's love for his nation got in the way, ultimately, leading to his death.

The woman would become, ill, with tuberculosis, which made her lose all hope, causing her to want to kill herself. Something made her keep going, however, which was the fact that the woman was going to give birth to a boy. She believed that she had lived an unfair, life, but just like her lover, she felt the need to fight for the boys' life. Eventually leading to her unfortunate demise just after her baby was born. Making her son the remaining member of her family's bloodline.

The theater gradually dimmed to complete darkness, and the music played by the orchestra became softer and more subdued. There was, however, one remaining light—focused on the baby—signaling the final act and the conclusion of the performance.

Once the show finished, the crowd gave the performers a huge standing ovation. The leader of the NEU, said a few words of encouragement, to the performers, who had been able to do a wonderful job.

A few moments later, the theater staff brought in a podium, where each of the designated members would deliver their messages to the assembled audience. Neither Liam nor Friedrich were there to speak; their role was to listen attentively to the speeches from representatives of other nations, focusing on discussions related to political, economic, and social issues affecting each country.

The members were not timed; therefore, they could take as long as they wanted to deliver their message. Each of the members were respectful, of each other's speech. This was particularly a good thing because out of the many countries, twenty were about to deliver their speech.

Each of the members, of the respective countries delivered their speech, in a very different way. The men discussed the negative, things about their country, but at the same time, each in every one of them delivered a beautiful message, as to why their country was moving in a positive direction. Once more the entire crowd applauded, acknowledging a well put together conference. Before the end, of the conference, the leader stepped on the stage one more time.

"Quite the conference, wasn't it." The NEU leader said.

"As we've all heard here today, their always up's and downs. But what we can't let happen, is let others decide our fate. I would like to share a personal anecdote –" the whole crowd was interested in the words of the leader.

"My country has had a very complicated history. The Russian people have had to endure the pain of politics, ideology, and change. All these things believed to make a positive impact, has brought us back in terms of our growth as a nation–" Liam would not say a word, but he found himself more focus, on what the leader had to say.

"We are a society that has been built on secrecy, and

discretion. Which some consider to be a double edge sword. You see, for years, our society has had an ongoing war, with the criminal organizations of our country. Fortunately, we have dealt with them successfully." No one reacted, but, Liam was proud to learn that the Russian, society was doing a good thing by preventing crime.

"Apart from, crime leaders, we have had a long war with, communist believers, who wish to dethrone us." As the leader of the NEU, was speaking, a group of men, most likely from the NEU, would roll a star into the stage.

"I agree, change is necessary. Today, I would like to take matter into my own hand." As Liam focused on the leader's speech, he did not notice a man tied to the star, which resembled the one featured on the Soviet flag.

"Today, I would like to do something unorthodox, are society requires change, that change begins know, here, with the most honorable men of each country." Liam would simply be engaged, to what was going on, that he did not pay attention to the crowd's reaction.

"As you know, in our society, there is no room, for traitors, the man on that star has been punishing my people. FOR YEARS!" the leader of the NEU, shouted angrily, expressing his anger towards the man.

"Our government has protected this man, They believe he has the right, to express his beliefs. What they don't know is that he is a manipulator, he uses the hopeless, to create change in our system." As he was finalizing his speech, a group of NEU members, would pour gasoline on the hopeless, man.

"This man is a symbol of the end. Our time has come to rise, higher than we have ever risen."

"May god rest his troubled soul." To finalize, the show, the NEU Members brought a handheld torch where the leader would simply toss it into the star.

As the man burned, he exhibited no signs of pain, which was due to the administration of a potent anesthetic by the NEU, designed to prevent any sensation of discomfort. This practice was both unusual and inhumane, as the man remained alive and conscious, fully aware of his impending death. As his body continued to burn, the lights suddenly went out, signaling the conclusion of the conference.

CHAPTER 4

NEW BEGININGS

Returning to the small town of Richmond Hill gave me a deep feeling of nostalgia. Six years passed; I was already 19 years old, and, although the surroundings remained practically unchanged, an intangible difference lingered in the air. The demanding but distinctive training imparted a wealth of lessons, the deepest insight being the ability to see life from a new perspective, inspiring meaningful reflection on the essence of existence. I arrived in the spring, when the flowers were in full bloom, representing to me a season of renewal and new beginnings. My father had chosen not to inform my mother of my return, opting instead to surprise her. As I headed to the dining room, I found my mother diligently sewing a jacket, probably for one of my younger cousins. I had been away for training several years earlier, and upon my arrival, my mother's joy was palpable. He immediately paused his work to embrace me warmly, reflecting his strength and depth of emotion at that moment. The intensity of her emotion prompted her to prepare a special meal to celebrate with my father.

My father's office had a strange ambiance to it. It had that aura of secrecy that also surrounded the Society. The moment we were about to share was definitely an important one. During this time, my father explained to me the significance of being a member. At the training, I wasn't told what our goal was. I was simply trained to see if I would fit the requirements to become a member of, perhaps, the most powerful society in the world. Our duty as members was to protect and serve the democracy of our country. We would deal with anything that could disrupt the freedom, peace, and well-being of the people on a much higher scale. Apart from our protection, we have control over everything in the country of Canada. Despite having differences in the way in which we operate, all the societies have the same level of control, making us the leaders of our nations in a very discreet manner.

My father informed me that every member plays a vital role within the society. For a nation to function effectively, there must be oversight by well-trained individuals who prioritize their country above all else. Each member has specific responsibilities, such as monitoring the economy to ensure operations run smoothly, while others are tasked with overseeing immigration to manage who enters and exits our country. The society was pleased to recognize my aptitude for working with computers and, as a result, expressed interest in having me join one of the largest cybersecurity firms in the world.

Out of all the things, returning home and sharing quality time with my family was something that I deeply cherished. My mother wanted to celebrate my graduation from the supposed advanced academy that I was at. After time had passed, and I grew older, wiser, and extremely disciplined, the trainer had let me sleep in one of the rooms inside the cabin. Nothing, however, could compare to sleeping in my room, with my soft and comfortable bed.

While at home with my parents, I couldn't help but inquire about what truly happened to Matt. As a member of the society, discretion was expected at all times, which made my father hesitant to answer. However, I persisted, explaining that the question had lingered in my mind ever since his passing. My father then explained that he was not an active member of the society but rather someone contracted by them. Matt was an artist with a vivid imagination; he was the individual responsible for forging documents on the society's behalf. In addition to document forgery, he was consulted for creating deceptive scenarios—a method the society employed to confuse potential enemies during covert operations. To conclude the conversation, my father revealed that the leader had decided to eliminate Matt because he had been working with a group of young men believed to hold dangerous political ideas. Matt was considered to possess sensitive knowledge about the society, and it was deemed necessary to end his life along with the information he possessed.

After a month, I commenced my employment at one of North America's leading cybersecurity firms, located in the vibrant heart of downtown Toronto. The interior design of the office was aesthetically pleasing, characterized by its modern architecture and immaculate cleanliness. Securing a position at such a prestigious organization was no small feat; however, I sensed an underlying reluctance within myself regarding this opportunity. As I stood in the midst of my colleagues—professionally attired men and women, much like myself—a woman approached me with a whiteboard to pose a question.

"Hi, how can I help?"

"Hi, I'm Charles. I'm looking for Mr. Romentel." I did not know why, but for some reason, the woman's pupils dilated.

"Oh, excuse me, but I don't see you on my list."

A clean-shaven man with a dark suit and blue tie suddenly appeared out of nowhere.

"It's fine, I will take it from here," the man with the blue tie said to the lady.

"I am Mr. Romentel. You must be Charles."

"Yes, sir."

"Good. Follow me."

Mr. Romentel and I walked towards the elevators.

The elevator doors opened simultaneously, and Mr. Romentel got out of the elevator before I did. We entered a spacious corridor where numerous individuals were engaged in computer work. Another hundred feet later, we reached a white door. Romentel opened it with a card he pulled out from his pocket. It led to a computer lab with two rows of computers where five young people were working diligently.

"Ladies and gentlemen, this is Charles; he will be joining you for the following weeks to come."

Everyone directed their attention towards me and welcomed me with open arms. Romentel gave me a slight pat on the back before leaving. I did not hesitate to take my seat at the end of the room. I knew a lot about cybersecurity, but I did not know what my task was. The only thing I knew was that I was getting put on trial like the rest of the people in the room. In the back of my head, I knew that I was most likely going to land a position in the company. The colleague next to me kindly gave me a sheet of paper with instructions on what I had to do. My role was to find out who the people behind the cyberattacks on a network of financiers are. Even if I had not attended college, unlike the rest of my colleagues, I never felt they were superior to me.

Before I began searching for who was responsible for the attacks, I drafted a plan on a blank sheet of paper I received from the printer next to me. I spent around one hour carefully planning how I was going to find the hackers. I dedicated the following two and a half hours to implementing the code on the software.

All my colleagues went to the cafeteria to grab some lunch. I was not hungry; I was more in the mood to step outside into the fresh air.

I was fortunate enough to find a seat isolated from the rest of the people. Stepping outside was the only thing that relieved me from the pressures I had been feeling since a young age. The natural sounds provided me with a great deal of peace that was much needed.

After relaxing outside the building, I came back into the lab, where most of my colleagues had returned to work. Something inside me did not feel right. All the young people were enthusiastic about getting this job, and I, on the other hand, was not very keen on it. I wanted to ask my colleagues how they were doing, as well as inform them that I was happy to assist them in any way possible. However, I was not like the rest of my peers; I had a bigger responsibility. I took some time to clear my mind before continuing with my work. For the rest of the time, I mostly did the same thing that I had done before my break. For the most part, the cyberattacks came from people who were as good or even better than we were. I thought maybe part of the reason the Society wanted me to work in this field was due to my analytical skills. The hours passed, and my colleagues slowly left the room. It took me a while to finish because I wanted to leave things planned out for the following day.

Returning home after a long day's work felt wonderful. I was still living with my parents, trying to make up for all the time we had lost as a family. My father was watching the television while my mother was in the kitchen cooking dinner for us. I went to give her a nice hug, which was well received.

"How was your first day?" my mother asked.

"Not bad at all, Mom. Although I must admit it feels quite strange."

She patted me on the back and said, "You will get used to it."

At the dining table, we had a great time sharing many old memories that made us all laugh. My mom's recipe was delicious, as always. My parents were tired and left the table before I did, which was something that had never occurred when I was younger. Many thoughts troubled me. The thought of sacrificing all that time so I could serve my country. Clearly, I understood the motives behind what I had to do, but that didn't mean it wasn't difficult for me to take in. It did not take me long to leave the table and prepare myself for yet another day at work.

A little over a week into my job, I began to accommodate myself to the work schedule. Despite it being a challenge, I managed to write temporary low-level protection software for all the companies that were under attack. It might not have been much, but it was enough to buy me some time while I built something more efficient.

A few seconds later, I was in the elevator, proud of what I had been able to achieve. On the first floor, I encountered Mr. Romentel, who informed me that there was something he wanted to discuss. We took the elevator without exchanging words. The floor where Mr. Romentel worked was protected by two security guards. The men checked me from top to bottom. After making sure I was clear, they let me pass. Mr. Romentel patiently waited on the other side. He was kind enough to lead me into his stunning office. What impressed me the most was the eye-catching skyline view he had from his desk. He poured me a glass of cold water.

"Thank you, sir," I said while he placed the glass on the table.

"How have your colleagues been treating you?" Mr. Romentel asked.

"Exceptionally well."

"You have managed to complete more work in a week than your colleagues in a month. That is something that not even the brightest of our men have been able to do."

"Luck was on my side, sir."

"No, what you have is skills that the rest do not have," Mr. Romentel said confidently. After a pause, he added, "You are not here just to receive compliments. One of your colleagues is trying to infiltrate our company. Your job is to find out who."

"Somebody wants to weaken our software." Charles asked, wanting to make sure his assumptions were true.

"Right on." Mr. Romentel quickly replied.

"Is it just one person?"

"We don't know yet; that is why we need you."

"You want me to spy on my colleagues."

"Yes. And we want you to do it in the most discreet way possible. Will you do it?"

"You can count on me," I replied, intending to look as confident as possible.

The revelation from Mr. Romentel gave me a lot to think about. I was quick to give him an answer because I didn't know if he was a member of the Canadian Society, putting me to the test.

One of the notable benefits of working at the company was the abundance of dining options available nearby. As I leisurely walked past several small eateries, I preferred not to sit down and wait for my meal to be prepared. Instead, I opted to visit a moderately busy sandwich shop. The establishment was well-maintained, and the soothing background music created a pleasant atmosphere conducive to relaxation and a temporary escape from work-related stresses. With various choices on the menu, I ultimately selected my favorite: the club sandwich. As I savored my meal, a striking young woman with brown hair approached my table, capturing my attention in an unforeseen manner.

"Mind if I join?"

"No, not at all," he said once he sat down. I stared into her emerald eyes, not knowing what to say.

She introduced herself as Jelena and offered me her hand. After exchanging some pleasantries about our food, she went on to tell me that she worked a few miles across the street as a sales representative for a local appliance store. I mentioned to her that I worked nearby because I wasn't allowed to talk about myself too much. Her conversation was so interesting that it kept me at the sandwich store way past my lunchtime. I took a brief look at my watch, but I was not rushed at all.

"I have to go, but it was a pleasure meeting you," she said when she finished her lunch.

I watched her leave and did not say a word to her. I comprehended that I was unable to be in any kind of relationship. Anyway, I decided to follow her. Something inside me told me that it was important to do so. She walked in the opposite direction from where I was heading. I did not have any idea about where her job was, exactly. She continued walking until she reached a random door. From afar, I took a look at her entering the building where she supposedly worked.

Entering the computer lab elicited an indescribable sensation. The realization that I was collaborating with an individual engaged in espionage while also operating in a similar capacity myself was a concept I struggled to comprehend. Despite this unsettling awareness, I maintained a façade of normalcy in my work. To further obscure my suspicions, I made the strategic decision to be the first to leave the building, thereby giving the impression that I was entirely unaware of the circumstances at hand.

Over the course of the next two months, my primary responsibility was not only to ascertain the identity of external attackers but also to pinpoint any internal individuals attempting to breach the company's security. The support and kindness exhibited by my colleagues made it increasingly challenging for me to fulfill this investigative role. By the third week, I began to question whether I was, in fact, the subject of scrutiny. The magnitude of the task was daunting, and it often felt as though I had little respite from my professional obligations. In my spare time, I diligently studied every detail about each of my five colleagues, meticulously documenting my observations in hopes of uncovering any clues. Despite my efforts, I was unable to identify any signs that could potentially shed light on the situation.

The fatigue from work led to an unfortunate incident of oversleeping one day. Had my mother not awakened me, I would have missed an entire day at work, which would have reflected poorly, as I felt both the company and the society were evaluating my commitment. My mother drew back the curtains, allowing sunlight to stream into the room. In my hurried state, I quickly made my way to the dining room, where I enjoyed a banana and a glass of orange juice. A few minutes later, I returned to my room to change and brush my teeth in preparation for the day ahead.

I drove downtown for about half an hour. When I got to the computer lab, only one of the trainees was working on the computer.

"What's going on here?"

He stopped what he was doing to look at me. "They all have failed their evaluation; only you and I remain."

I could not help but think that either almost the whole team was infiltrated or that this was a test for me to try to determine if the last remaining person was indeed the spy. Either way, I continued with my daily tasks as usual. That day, we both decided to have lunch together. I agreed because the more I spoke with him, the more I would learn about him.

It was my first time in the cafeteria. It was quite impressive, filled with various healthy food choices, along with very comfortable tables to sit at. I had my own packed lunch, but I joined my colleague to take a closer look at the food they had. It was astonishing the amount of food that they had to offer; it was fresh and well-kept. However, what really caught my eye was the beautiful and modern soda machine. Just for the sake of it, I got a nice cold soft drink. After my colleague had chosen his drink, we sat at a table at the far end.

"My name is Tim, by the way."

I nodded and answered, "Charles."

We engaged in a thoughtful discussion covering various topics. He expressed a particular interest in understanding my motivation for selecting a career in cybersecurity. I provided a foundational response, but the truth was that I was unsure of my reasons for pursuing this field beyond the society's encouragement for me to become a cybersecurity agent and my innate aptitude for the discipline. He proceeded to share the challenges he had faced to reach his current position. I found his journey to be both compelling and inspiring; it highlighted the significant sacrifices one must make to achieve a single goal. This conversation was arguably the most enriching interaction I had experienced with anyone in the company. We enjoyed our exchange so much that we exceeded our one-hour lunch break.

Walking back to the lab, an unpleasant welcome awaited Tim and me: the middle-aged, cyclothymic supervisor. We didn't say a word, I out of respect and Tim out of concern that he wouldn't get the job.

"What have you two been doing?" asked the supervisor. I had a lot of training on reading body language and could see that Tim was afraid.

"We miscalculated lunchtime, sir."

He looked at us for a few seconds without saying a word.

"Work's due in a week." He slammed the door, kind of mildly, but enough to let us know that he had left not in the happiest of moods. I focused on the worried Tim.

"Let's get to work."

I started on the easiest task, just to get it out of the way.

We stayed in the lab until after seven o'clock. Neither of us had any gas left in the tank, so we decided to call it a day. Before leaving, I grabbed a book from the shelf nearby to check something that was worrying me about my job.

I arrived home, where my father was watching the local news in the living room. He turned the television off as soon as he saw me.

"Someone was busy today."

"Just trying to do my best."

"I've heard there have been troubles concerning the company."

I wasn't sure if my father was referring to Mr. Romentel's specific mission.

"Is that uncommon?" I asked.

"I guess not," my father replied, staring into my eyes.

The following morning, I woke up earlier than usual, having so many work-related things to do.

I dressed up in my office attire, had a quick breakfast, and left home.

It was fairly early, so when I arrived at the building, barely anyone was present. I headed straight to the elevator, where an elderly man dressed in a gray suit stood beside me. When I reached my floor, I stepped out and extended my sincerest wishes to the gentleman before proceeding to the computer lab, which was currently closed. Nobody was nearby, so I immediately reacted, going to the first floor.

The receptionist was working on her computer. I interrupted her to kindly ask for the keys to the computer lab. She checked all the drawers, but they were nowhere to be found. She looked hesitant and confused.

"Looking for these?" I heard my supervisor say while showing us the keys. "Come with me; there are things I want to talk to you about."

We went to the supervisor's office. It was very early in the morning, but he poured himself a glass of whiskey. He respectfully offered me a glass, which I declined because I did not believe it was appropriate to drink before work, even though I was already 19 years old and could have accepted it.

"It's a celebratory day; you should definitely have something to drink."

I did not know what to think exactly.

"What is the motive for the celebration, sir?"

"You have earned yourself a position in the company." I was happy to have gotten the job, but there was still something in my mind.

"What about Tim? What happened to him?" I asked while he was looking at his monitor.

"Whatever happened to him is neither my nor your problem," the supervisor responded in a very relaxed manner.

"You have performed better than any other trainee. The committee has decided whom we want to work for our company."

Although I had declined an alcoholic beverage, the cyclothymic supervisor handed me a glass of whiskey. He held his glass up high, offering a toast, and I clinked my glass out of respect for him. The supervisor gave me a brief overview of what my daily job would be like.

After the small celebration, the supervisor led me to my office. It was not spacious, but it was well maintained, and the air conditioning worked like magic. But what caught my attention was the eye-catching scenery of the buildings that I had from my desk.

"With a view like this, anyone would be motivated," the supervisor said, acknowledging the stunning view from my office. "Good luck, Charles," he added before exiting my office.

Proudly, I sat on my chair and checked my inbox to catch up with my daily tasks. Luckily for me, the workload was not much. I decided to take the day off because I did not have much work to do.

On the way to my car, I spotted the girl that I had met the other day. I didn't think she would see me because my car was in the opposite direction to where she was heading. I wanted to avoid her, but we crossed paths as I was ready to get in my car.

"Charles! What a surprise!"

"Yeah, what a surprise," I replied with more dishonesty than complacency towards her presence.

"Am I holding you back?" Jelena asked.

"No, well... it's just that I have a time-sensitive matter to attend to," I replied.

"Oh, I see... Shall we exchange numbers?" Jelena asked confidently.

"Sure," I replied, eager to take my path. She handed me her phone, where I quickly put my number in.

"Alright, I will text you sometime," Jelena said before walking away.

I needed to unwind, so I decided to drive to a local park. There I sat on a bench with a notebook and a pen and started writing about myself and the different people I had met. This was something I learned with the trainer. Evaluating one's behavior is as important as evaluating other people's behavior. Everything was in check, except Jelena; something seemed strange about her. Her ambiguous personality, along with her dazzling green eyes, might have been what caught my attention.

The sound of nature is something that will never get old, in my opinion. Different memories come to mind; this makes time go rapidly. I checked my watch, and it was 12:30, making it the right time to go get some lunch.

Adjacent to our location, there was a charming boulevard featuring various restaurants. After reviewing the menus of several establishments, I opted to dine at a seafood restaurant. The interior was distinctive, adorned with nautical decor, including anchors and images of various beaches and fishermen. The ambiance was tranquil and inviting, providing a pleasant environment for dining. I perused the menu to determine my meal selection.

"Hello, my name is Sarah. What can I get you to drink?" The middle-aged waitress asked.

"Yes, I would like a glass of cold water"

"No problem."

The woman returned in a blur to ask about my food.

"Have you decided what you would like, sir?"

"Yes, I would like a creamy clam chowder soup."

"Anything else?"

"No, that would be all for now."

While I waited for my soup, I tried to do some research about Jelena on my phone using her number. But I couldn't find anything, which was, in fact, something worrying. The waitress came with the plate of hot soup shortly after I had put my phone away. The soup was delectable and perfectly cooked to my preference.

The lady stopped by to inquire if I needed anything else. I was pretty full. Therefore, I didn't want anything. She insisted and handed me a dessert menu. I took a brief look, hoping to find something interesting, but I was unable to find an option that would suit my personal preferences. The lady came back, and I told her that there were suitable options, but I was not in the mood. She politely took the menu away and brought me my bill. Although the soup was not expensive at all, I tipped her fifty dollars for her kind service. At first, she was hesitant to accept, but I persuaded her to retain them.

Before heading home, I stopped at the athletic club my father used to take me to when I was young. The place had changed a bit since then; however, the luxurious nature of the place was still present. A young man, who was sitting at the circular counter, greeted me kindly and got ready to scan my membership.

"I would like a daily pass." I said, Not being a member of the club.

"Sure, that will be forty dollars," the man at the counter replied.

I pulled out my wallet and swiped my credit card on the payment machine. The man handed me my receipt.

The place was not busy, most likely because it was the middle of the day and because the club charged costly rates. It was perfect for me. I returned to my car to get changed, but I had no spare clothes. I had no other choice but to buy a towel, a T-shirt, and swimming shorts in the gift shop inside the club. Afterward, I went into the large, luxurious bathroom to get changed. I hadn't been to the club for such a long time that I had forgotten where to find the pool. Luckily, there were signs around I could follow.

The interior was fully changed, although it remained as luxurious as it was years ago; only it was a bit more modern. The blue LED light stripes on the wall made it the ideal place to relax. I dove right into the pool and went for a swim. Time flew by. In the best of moods, I walked up the stairs of the pool to dry myself off. On my way out, there were three Society members dressed casually standing before me.

"Is there a problem, gentlemen?" I asked them.

"We need you to come with us, if you do not mind." The member in the middle said. I simply nodded, letting them know that I was open to joining them.

CHAPTER 5

THE INITIATION

The society members led me to a black SUV, where I sat in the rear seat. I knew where they were going to take me, but I couldn't be 100% sure. During the journey, the sole option available to me was to maintain a calm demeanor and exhibit patience. The trip was long, but not bad at all, given that we did not run into traffic along the way. Being sat at the back, it was hard for me to guess where the men were heading, especially because there was a large black glass preventing me from hearing or seeing the members. Finally, the car made a full stop.

Training had taught me to trust my instincts, which is precisely what I did. It took a while for the men to open the door on my side. Once they fully opened the door, I exited the car without any issue whatsoever. One of the members led me to the front, where my dad was standing. At the time, I couldn't understand what exactly was going on. Until that very moment, I had never seen such a proud look in my father's eyes.

I could not help but ask, "Is there something wrong?"

He looked at me before answering, "Quite the opposite."

He hugged me, confirming that he was indeed proud of me.

We stepped inside the large home of the Canadian leader, where I had already been before. My father walked alongside me. He had said that I would have the ceremony later that night, but for now, I had to do something important.

One commonality shared by all the societies is their use of Venetian masks. This longstanding tradition serves as an enigmatic symbol of the secrecy that permeates our existence. The masks function not only to conceal our identities but also as a means for members to articulate the importance of discretion. Once again, I found myself in a meeting with the leader of the Canadian Society. Upon my arrival at his spacious yet elegantly appointed office, I observed him engaged in a phone conversation. The office was exactly as one might expect—meticulously organized and featuring a design that was both traditional and refined. I settled into a plush chair that provided exceptional comfort, patiently awaiting the conclusion of the leader's discussion.

"I am guessing, by now, you know why you are here," the Canadian leader stated in a sort of cheerful mood.

"With all due respect, sir, I barely know who I am."

The Canadian leader looked at me with a slight smile on his face before getting up from his seat.

"Today is a big day for you, Charles."

He pulled a briefcase from a cabinet and unlocked it with a key. He took his seat and opened the box he had for me. My eyes could not believe what I was witnessing; inside were three beautiful Venetian masks that caught my attention.

"This is one of our beautiful symbols. Each of the masks has a different meaning. The mask you choose will describe your character."

For me, it was incredibly difficult to process that a Venetian mask could have any sort of meaning. At the time, I did not know whether the Canadian leader was testing me or not, so I decided to take my time to pick the right mask. All the masks had red and white colors, which was because we were in Canada, and we represented the Canadian Society.

Each mask was adorned with genuine diamonds, contributing to their high value. The first mask featured a predominance of red, accentuated by a scattering of diamonds, while the second mask achieved a harmonious balance of color on either side, organized horizontally rather than vertically. My personal favorite was the third mask, which eschewed red almost entirely, showcasing a pristine white surface embellished with numerous ruby-colored diamonds. The atmosphere during the selection process was notably tense for reasons I could not pinpoint. After meticulously evaluating all my options, I lifted my gaze to focus on the Canadian leader.

"Have you decided?" the Canadian leader asked.

I looked at the box one more time. All the options were great, but it was hard not to pick the third one, my favorite one. I took the mask out of the box while the Canadian leader looked at me, not surprised at all.

"A man of power and justice, something that is vital to the Society. This mask should be taken care of as if your life depended on it."

The mask felt so good in my hands; it almost felt as if some form of power was handed to me suddenly.

"All the members will gather tonight; there will be a ceremony where you will be recognized as a member. Keep the box. All the masks are yours, but remember to wear the mask that you have chosen to the ceremony. The members deserve to know your choice."

The leader's presence commanded my full attention, emphasizing the significance of his directives. He pressed a small bell located next to his telephone, prompting one of the Canadian team members to graciously open the door for me. With the box in hand, I exited the room, accompanied by the Canadian representative, who escorted me to my father. Upon arrival, he congratulated me and expressed his pride in my accomplishments.

I had left my car at the club. Therefore, my father drove me back. Something seemed off at the time. However, I could not tell what it was. It took me some time to realize that the Society was not worried that I knew their location, probably because I was already a member. After a pleasant ride, sharing moments we spent together at the club when I was a kid, we arrived at our destination fairly quickly. I did not see the car I had parked by the entrance of the club. I turned to my father, confused. He parked in the first available spot. With the beautiful platinum box in my hand, I stepped out of the car a bit confused. I knew where I had parked my car, but for some strange reason, it was not there.

"Something wrong?" my father asked, most likely judging by the look on my face.

"Yeah, I don't see my car."

My father did not reply; instead, he made intense eye contact with me.

"Did that car have any meaning to you?"

"Of course, it is my means of transport," I answered the odd question.

"Hopefully, an upgrade wouldn't bother you."

My father turned his attention to the white, four-door

luxury car parked in the spot next to his. At the time, I did not feel like I was deserving of such a prize. My father tossed me the keys, confirming what he had suggested.

"Why don't you check it out?" my father said, in a great mood.

I proudly gave him a wide smirk before walking towards the car. I did not waste time turning on the engine from the outside. You wouldn't even know if the car was on because the engine of the brand-new car did not make any noise. The inside of the car had that fresh smell that every new car has. All the interior designs were immaculate; everything was beautiful. After letting me enjoy all the perks that the car had to offer, my father honked his horn from a distance. I stuck my hand out of the window to give him one last goodbye. The car had such advanced features that I had to get familiar with them before I headed back home. After a few minutes, I adjusted my seat and left the club. The car had such smooth movement, it did not feel like I was driving a car.

I arrived home excited but hungry at the same time. My mother was not around, and my father was at the mansion with the rest of the society members. Standing in the kitchen, I could not help but wonder if my mother even slightly suspected what my father and I were involved in. The fridge was empty. I decided to take the lonely lime soda on the top shelf of the fridge. I sat on the living room couch all by myself. It was crazy to think how peaceful the house was without the commotion of others. I was hesitant to activate the television, as it would have disrupted the tranquil atmosphere within the premises. Sitting on the couch, I could only think about what the initiation to the Society would be like. It was only a matter of time before my phone began to vibrate in my pocket. I grabbed it, just in case it was something important. It was a message from my father.

"Charles, please open the trunk of the car; your attire for the ceremony is inside."

I drank my last sip of soda before heading outside.

The outside was quiet and clear of any cars or pedestrians. I opened my trunk to find a beautiful, polished brown box. I grabbed the box and headed back into the house. Inside the box, there was a beautiful dark suit. I don't know why, but the material felt good. The suit did not have much to it, apart from a small badge with the symbol of the Society. I took another look at the box, just in case there was something else inside. The only thing that was inside was an 18-karat gold necklace with the same symbol that was on the suit.

I glanced at the vintage clock mounted on the wall, confirming that I was on schedule. Opting for a quick, warm shower to refresh myself, I was acutely aware of the anxiety surrounding the prospect of oversleeping, which prompted me to forgo a nap. Instead, I reached for a book I had been reading on the nightstand next to my bed, seeking to calm my nerves before one of the most significant moments of my life. Reading had been a valuable habit I had cultivated even before my training; regardless of genre, it provided a mental exercise that no other pastime could replicate. This day had, perhaps, been one of the most enjoyable I had experienced in quite some time. The engrossing book about lions captivated my attention to such an extent that I lost track of time. It was only when a twinge of thirst prompted me to check the clock that I realized the initiation was in approximately one and a half hours, and I had yet to don my dark suit.

I put everything else on hold. Luckily for me, the suit was nicely ironed. I took a look at the suit before putting it on. It was surprising, knowing that the suit fit me perfectly. Before leaving, I grabbed my Patek Philippe watch.

I made a stop just outside the house before entering back inside. The weather outside was actually colder than I had expected it to be. Quickly, I headed towards my room and put on a dark burgundy-colored overcoat. I finally exited the house and got inside my car. The car was ready to go since I had started it while I was getting ready.

Prepared to depart, I recalled that I had started this journey while getting ready. The location I was driving to was not the opulent mansion I had visited on several occasions; rather, I was headed to a modest fragrance store. As members of the Society, direct access to the sacred temple—where pivotal events occur—was prohibited to protect the sanctity of our most cherished location. Throughout Toronto, there were numerous entrance points to the temple, and fortunately, my modern vehicle was equipped with GPS, which would guide me to the precise location. The weather was cold, and traffic was minimal, allowing me to arrive at the fragrance store in approximately thirty minutes. Finding a parking space was relatively easy since the shop was closed—an unusual occurrence given the hour. A few pedestrians meandered by, and while I experienced no overt nervousness, I felt an inexplicable hesitation to step outside. As I was not yet an official member, I remained uncertain if the society was subjecting me to one final evaluation. Exercising considerable patience, I waited until the sidewalk was as clear as possible before retrieving my mask and exiting the vehicle.

The wind was not intense, but it was present. I put my hands in my pockets because I feared dropping my mask on my way in. The store was closed, but it did not matter; my dad had told me where I could find the keys. Before opening the store, I slowly scanned the area, making sure nobody was spying on me.

Much to my surprise, I was able to unlock the door fairly quickly. I shut the door immediately after entering the store. There was little to no visibility inside, and I did not turn on the lights because I had been given clear instructions not to. It did not take me long to reach the back room. where I could turn on the lights once I closed the door, confirming outside pedestrians were unable to see from the inside.

The back room was small, filled with multiple boxes. I had to find out what box I had to open. I paused for a second. To check each one of them, in hopes of finding something that would make one stand out from the rest of the boxes. Even though I was against the clock, I did not have any other option than to fill myself up with patience.

In the midst of poor visibility and surrounded by countless boxes, the task at hand resembled searching for a needle in a haystack. I successfully identified a specific box that stood out due to the company's logo. Eagerly, I opened the box, hoping it contained what I sought. Inside, I discovered a mold designed to fit perfectly with the mask I had selected earlier. I took the mask mold and positioned it against the wall, then placed my mask in position. This action initiated the mechanism, causing the walls to slide apart, revealing a set of concrete stairs that led to an un-known destination. Before descending, I donned my mask. As I entered, the doors closed automatically behind me. Despite my efforts to maintain professionalism through-out the process, I found it challenging to suppress my as-tonishment at the events that had transpired thus far. The rapid beating of my heart echoed in the silence, amplifying a blend of confusion, fear, and excitement.

I walked down the stairs, where the halls stretched and the walls were lit by flame torches. Given all the circumstances, it was incredibly difficult to see. Nevertheless, I kept walking to the end, where a Canadian member wearing a plain white mask was waiting for me. He bowed his head, most likely to pay his respects to a new member. I bowed my head, not knowing what to do. The masked Canadian member led me to a door. While walking towards our destination, we did not speak a word to each other at all. The Canadian member knocked gently on the door. It was only a matter of time before two other members, wearing similar masks, opened the door for us. The Canadian member with the plain white mask gestured for me to go in front of him.

Judging by the small entrance, I would have never guessed the massive nature of the temple. The members of the society, all wearing beautiful masks, were sitting on the sides. I was in the middle, walking on a narrow red carpet. The Leader was at the far end, wearing a white and gold mask, along with a crown, standing at the pulpit. All the members took a seat on the pew, while I took a knee in front of my leader.

"Gentlemen, today we are going to introduce a new member into our society."

The temple could not have been any more silent.

"Today, he will swear his life and loyalty in front of all the members of the society."

I remained on my knees, not knowing what to do.

"Please, rise and face your fellow members," the leader said while referring to me. I did exactly as I was told. The members were separated by the color of their masks; the ones who wore white masks were on the right, while the ones wearing red were on the left.

"Please repeat after me," the Canadian leader said. "I shall defend my country at all costs."

I followed the orders of the Canadian leader and repeated his words every time he made a statement.

"I shall sacrifice myself for the Society when the moment arises."

"There will be no barrier, no setback, no complication that will stop me from protecting my society."

I repeated the exact words that the leader had told me to repeat.

"I swear my loyalty not only to my society but to my country, which shall always be free of tyranny."

"Now, turn around."

I did as I was told.

"Please, take a seat," the Canadian leader said, referring to the majestic chair that looked similar to a throne.

The nerves caused a slight hesitation before walking towards the chair. Nevertheless, my leader had requested me to take a seat, and that is precisely what I did. The chair was very comfortable and had enough space for me to move around freely. All the members were lined up in a straight line. Until now, it was one of the most awkward moments in my life, given that I had not done much to deserve praise from the rest of the members. All the members kissed me on my hand while on their knees. It took nearly an hour for the initiation to be officially done; there were numerous members moving at a slow pace. Only I and the members who were standing by the door remained in the temple. Some Canadian members, who I could not identify, slowly shut the door.

The Canadian leader, who still had his mask on, asked to follow him. The moment was unique and beautiful, but I wanted to leave the place to go home. I followed the leader to the back of the temple, where there was a small rectangular table. The leader took a seat. He removed his mask before telling me that it was fine for me to do so. I took my mask off even though it was not bothering me. The leader took a sip of water, already on the table.

"Congratulations, Charles, I can officially call you a member."

"Thank you, sir," I answered out of great respect for the leader of my country.

"Things will be different, I'm sure you know that."

"I am ready for anything, sir."

I did not hesitate to demonstrate that I was willing to do anything to serve the Society.

"After you finished your training, Birkir, the man who trained you, retired from the Society."

I looked into the eyes of the leader, not having a clue as to where the conversation was heading.

"We suspect he is passing classified information to the leader of the NEU."

"The NEU?" I asked, not knowing what the leader was talking about.

"The NEU, also known as the Northern European Union, is a society just like ours. The only difference is that they have joined forces with countries that have common interests."

It was my first day as a member, and I had no idea what the leader was talking about.

"They believe in totalitarianism, a form of power that is too extreme even for people like us."

The Canadian leader, gladly, gave me his explanation.

"What about us? What form of government do we believe in?" I asked, not knowing if the question was worthy of an answer.

"Even though we hold absolute power over our countries, we cannot come to terms with extreme public ideologies. That has been one of the many reasons great empires have fallen."

I would watch as the leader of my society took another sip of water.

"I need you to wiretap Birkir's house, your old trainer. Please do this for me."

Even though he was a powerful leader, he had asked me to do it so humbly.

"I am at your service, sir," I replied.

"Good to hear."

Out of nowhere, a masked member joined us and took a seat.

"I have arranged a flight for you to Iceland. The stewardess will provide you with an envelope that contains all the information. Have I made myself clear?" the Canadian leader asked, wanting to make sure I was indeed paying attention?

"Crystal clear, sir."

"This member will show you the way."

Before rising from my chair, I took my mask. The Canadian member who was still wearing his mask led me through the beautiful Society temple. This time, the way I left was different from the way I came in. The other member and I proceeded towards a diminutive chamber that appeared to be a library. It was strange because the member would not talk while checking all the books neatly stacked on wooden shelves. It did not take long for the member to find the exact book he was looking for. I was impressed by the fact that he could find any book, given that they were all the same color and had the same society symbol.

He turned a couple of pages before grabbing the modern lamp that was nearby. The lamp changed from a warm color to a much cooler color. He carefully lit the book for about two minutes before closing it and putting it back on the shelf.

Suddenly, the Canadian member left my side. It was all

so new and confusing to me. The bookshelves parted. For some reason, I was still impressed to see how much the Society valued the power of secrecy. The Canadian member walked towards the parted shelves before gesturing with his hand for me to go first. I did not hesitate and did as I was told because he had better status in the society than I did. The stairs were identical to the ones I took to enter the beautiful temple. Walking down the stairs, I had to be a little more careful because of how dark it was. It took me a while to go down the numerous stairs. I had finally reached the bottom, where there was a small train car.

From a short distance, I was able to hear the walls closing behind me. Shortly after, the Canadian member descended the stairs, approaching my location.

"Take a seat," the member said.

I positioned myself at the rear of the train, while the Canadian representative took his place at the front to oversee our journey. With a firm push on the long lever, the train gradually began to accelerate. Fortunately, I had worn my overcoat, as the temperature in the underground environment was quite chilly. As the train gained considerable speed, my surroundings became a mere blur. After navigating several sharp turns, the train eventually came to a complete stop. The Canadian representative struggled momentarily with the lever to ensure that the train remained stationary. His communication was predominantly non-verbal; he gestured with his hands more than he spoke. Extending his hand towards me, he wished me luck for the challenges that lay ahead. I looked into his eyes, despite the obscurity of his features, and confidently shook his hand, feeling a sense of pride at that moment.

Once the Canadian member left, I stood in front of the black door, not knowing what to expect. I opened the door, which led to a small office. I looked around the office, wondering if I was in the right place. The lights inside that particular room were dark, and the blinds were closed. I looked around to try to figure out where I was.

A random man entered the room and said, "Charles, please come with me."

I looked at the man, confused, but listened to him nonetheless. I walked through the empty office alongside the man. It was not until I reached the outside that I finally figured out where I was.

I was at an executive airport. I found it difficult to understand how in the world I had ended up in a place so significantly far from my location. Anyway, I had to remain focused on the task ahead of me, which was not easy at all.

The man led me to the hangar, where a Gulfstream G500 was waiting for me. The little that I knew about planes, I learned it from the trainer. Multiple employees of the executive airport attached the airstairs to the plane's fuselage. It was my first mission, and it was a bit nerve-racking. However, I was excited to get on the plane.

"Safe flight, Charles," is what the man, whose name I

did not know, said before leaving my side.

Slowly, I walked up the stairs, where a beautiful Middle Eastern stewardess was waiting for me. Out of respect, I greeted her on my way into the plane. The inside was how I imagined it: compact but luxurious. I sat down on the first seat I found. Once the airstairs were removed, the plane left the hangar and went onto the runway, where it would get ready to take flight.

I took off my overcoat to be more comfortable inside the plane. The plane finally took flight, with the smoothest takeoff I had ever experienced. At a steady pace, it ascended further into the air. I laid back in my seat, aiming to relax, before heading on what looked like a very difficult mission. It took a little over half an hour for the plane to settle on its altitude. It was dark and cloudy. Therefore, I had no reason to slide open the shade of the window.

"Would you like anything to drink, sir?"

"Yes, I will have a regular gin and tonic, please."

"Right away," the kind lady replied before leaving my side.

The stewardess promptly returned with my gin and tonic, to which I expressed my gratitude with a subtle nod.

"Anything else?"

"No, I'm fine for now," I answered, just wanting some time for myself.

"That's good. My boss has ordered me to hand you this."

The lady placed the envelope on the small table, next to where I had placed my gin.

A flight from Canada to Iceland was indeed a very long one. I wanted to enjoy my time on the plane because I didn't know when I would have another opportunity to get on a luxury plane like this one. The air was cool, and to my surprise, there was not much turbulence. The plane had plenty of magazines included, and I picked one up from the table that was next to me. The magazine covered many things from the entertainment industry, which I happened to know little about. After briefly skimming through the pages, I finished my drink. The stewardess came at the same time, I politely declined anything else. I made sure that she had left the area before checking the envelope.

From the outside, the material in the envelope did not look like it had much. I carefully opened it, not wanting to damage whatever might be inside. I opened the folded paper, which had all the details of my former trainer. He did not speak much, and when he did, it was solely to give commands. There were countless sheets because the type of paper used was very thin. The information was mostly about how my trainer, Birkir, was speaking with different members from the NEU. The envelope also included background information about the members he had been speaking to.

The last sheet contained information on the mission. All the peace that I had inside my head was gone all of a sudden. The Society wanted me to skydive out of the plane. My landing spot would be a village where Birkir had been living for the past few months. It seemed ironic that I was going to spy on the same man who trained me to be a member of the Society. There was still some time left to arrive at my destination, so I decided to take a quick nap to prepare myself for the big task that was ahead of me.

Despite not being too keen about sleeping on a plane in constant motion, it was all I had, and it is precisely what I took. I woke up after two hours and got up from the chair to stretch a little bit. The stewardess came to ask, "Would you like a glass of water, sir?"

"Yes, please."

She immediately left to bring me a glass of water. I opened the top compartment to find a bag with the wing-suit I was going to be using. The kind stewardess interrupted me to hand me a glass of cold water.

"Thank you; you have been incredibly kind."

I made sure to tell her that her service had been spectacular before I had to jump out of the plane. While hydrating myself, I examined the material of the wingsuit, which was quite light and stretchy. Once more, I took a look at the exact spot I had to land at. We were approximately one hour away, not much, but I was not rushed.

Half an hour had gone by. I went to the back of the plane to get changed. Judging from the outside, you would think that the bathroom is much larger. But it wasn't a problem because there was enough room for me to get changed. Before exiting, I made sure to fold the clothes I used for the initiation.

The time I had to jump out of the plane was slowly shrinking. I took a look at the last sheet of the information on where I had to land. The instructions said to land on the Kirkjufell peninsula, on a circle made of green flares. I was not afraid. However, it was impossible not to be nervous. Once more, the stewardess came to me to ask if I needed help with something.

"I just want you to take care of my things for me." I told her.

"No problem, sir, I am here to help."

I stood up from my chair for two reasons: first, to stretch, and second, to alleviate some of my nervousness. After approximately ten minutes, I decided to approach the emergency exit. As I had only ten minutes remaining before the jump, I still grappled with lingering hesitation. To ensure that my actions would not disrupt the operations of the flight crew, I informed the pilot of my intentions. I then proceeded to knock on the door separating the cockpit from the passenger cabin.

"How may we help you?" were the words that came out of the pilot's mouth once opening the door.

"I am not sure if you are aware, but I'm going to use the emergency exit in a few minutes."

The pilot looked back into the cockpit before answering.

"Everything seems to be fine," the pilot said, confused.

"I know, but I have my orders."

"As you wish, then," the pilot replied.

"Can you tell me our altitude?"

The pilot turned his head to check.

"We are approximately at twenty-five thousand feet."

"I need you to descend at a height of fifteen thousand feet."

"Will do, sir," were the last words of the pilot before I left.

Back at the emergency door, I counted to ten before opening the door. The wind was rough, although I disregarded all the possible negative outcomes.

Even the most professional skydivers would be frightened to do what I did. It was dark and gloomy, as well as windy. In those conditions, it was difficult to maneuver in the direction I wanted to go. It was worrying that I continued to descend and still could not control myself in the air. I was finally able to control the direction I was heading at around a third of the way to where I was supposed to land.

Fortunately for me, I figured out what direction I needed to go. It was not too long before I would spot the circle of green flares. Once I was at the right altitude, I released my parachute. By the time that happened, I was already calm and collected. My intuition told me not to relax too much because I was unsure if the man who was going to pick me up was a member of the Canadian Society. I calculated the direction and strength of the wind to land in the middle of the circle.

I was so focused on my task that I had forgotten how beautiful the surrounding scenery was. Even though it was pitch black, the beauty of the Kirkjufell peninsula was undeniable. I put my parachute back in the bag before walking outside the circle. The place was as anyone would have expected it to be: large and desolate. The files on the envelope had clearly stated that there would be a man waiting for me inside a white jeep. However, there was nobody around. It was not until after ten minutes that the white jeep arrived.

Something was completely off; the driver was my old trainer himself.

"Well, what a surprise!" Birkir, the man who had trained me, said.

"I guess the feeling is mutual," I replied.

"Are you going to hop on, or would you like to sleep the night out in the cold?"

I decided to take the ride with my former trainer, given that I did not have much of a choice. There was no clear path, and the weather was indeed severely cold.

"So, what brings you here?" Birkir asked. I did not know whether he was being sarcastic or not.

"The Society wants me to wiretap your home."

I told him the truth because I knew my trainer more than my father. He was one of the smartest men that I had ever met.

"They just can't leave me alone, can they?"

"The leader told me you were working for the NEU."

"Is that what they are saying about me?" Birkir bluntly replied.

"What is happening?" I asked.

"It's a long story."

It did not take long to arrive at the micro village my trainer called home. Birkir lived in a small house, far away from the rest of the population. The house was different from the one that I had trained at, but it brought me memories of the time I spent training. The inside was not much, but at least it was something.

"Take a seat; I'll get you something to drink," Birkir said while walking towards his kitchen.

I examined the area before sitting on the couch. Thankfully, the place was warm, which was a good thing given how extreme the weather was outside. Birkir came back with two cups of hot chocolate. I was not a huge hot chocolate fan. However, I accepted it with open arms. We both took a sip of the hot chocolate; it was actually pretty good.

"Now that we are safe, I need you to give me an in-depth explanation of what the Society has said about me," Birkir said, intending to plan his next move.

"All they told me was they needed me to wiretap your house because you were speaking with members of the NEU."

"Did they ask you to kill me?" Birkir asked calmly and confidently.

"No."

I was not hesitant to reply.

Birkir took a minute to look around the house before taking a small sip of the hot chocolate. I, on the other hand, would not do anything else but stare into his eyes.

"How long did they give you?" Birkir asked, referring to my mission.

"Just a few days."

"You know what they want from you, don't you?"

"It is difficult to believe, if it is what I am thinking," I replied, knowing exactly what was going through my trainer's head.

"The fact that it is difficult to grasp does not make it false."

"Even if I am indeed a member, I would never do something I believe to be unethical."

"We will need to prepare ourselves then, but for now, get some rest."

Birkir grabbed his cup of hot chocolate before leaving the area.

I found myself in the small, yet cozy living room. It had been an incredibly stressful day. I lay on the couch and went to sleep.

The sun was slightly out when I woke up the following morning. After around six hours, I had safely recharged my energy. From the looks of it, Birkir had been up for a while.

"How did you sleep?" Birkir asked.

"Comfortably."

"Good."

"Is it true that you have been working with the NEU?" I asked, wanting to get additional information out of Birkir.

"Retired people do not work, Charles. However, from time to time, we do assist the ones we consider loyal."

"You have friends in the NEU?" I asked.

"Of course. We were all very close to each other."

"What went wrong?"

"Our differences. They made us distance ourselves," he said, while I carefully paid attention.

"There is no choice for me but to protect myself. You are proof that they are coming after me. I need you to visit an old friend." Birkir said.

"This friend of yours, is he linked to the Society in any way?"

"Yes, but he is not a member. He has long been the man who fabricates our weapons."

"Does the Society know where he lives?"

Birkir looked at me with a smirk on his face.

"No. Only I do."

"Now, will you make my life simpler and come with me?"

I paused for a second before nodding once.

"I will be waiting for you."

I rose from the sofa and proceeded to the bathroom to wash my face and brush my teeth. I completed my preparations in a timely manner. Outside, Birkir was attending to the car engine. After shutting the door, I approached him as he settled into the driver's seat. While the atmosphere within the jeep was calm, our conversation was minimal during the journey. I had no cause for complaint, as this experience had been one of the most remarkable car rides I had ever enjoyed. Canada is renowned for its stunning landscapes; however, the unparalleled natural beauty of Iceland—characterized by frozen lakes and breathtaking waterfalls—was truly unmatched. Birkir resided in such a remote area that it took us nearly an hour and a half to reach the nearest village.

As we entered the small town, Birkir parked the jeep in front of a quaint, two-story wooden house painted a deep red, nestled by the tranquil lake. Its weathered exterior gave off an air of abandonment, but I couldn't shake the feeling I might be mistaken; the other houses around us shared the same ghostly stillness. Birkir ascended the creaking stairs, and I scanned the surroundings, wary of any curious eyes lurking nearby. With a sense of urgency, he knocked firmly on the door. After a tense moment, an old man resembling Matt appeared, his face lined with age and wisdom. He stepped aside, gesturing for us to enter his home.

The interior was very gloomy and rustic, with carpet floors with a peculiar smell I could not identify. We all sat on the couch.

"The evidence is clear," Birkir said.

The old man took a closer look at me.

"Has it really come down to this?" the old man replied.

"I don't make the decisions," Birkir quickly replied.

"Have my payment ready; my work begins once you leave my home."

It took a while to respond, but the old man finally came to terms.

It did not take long before we left that strange house. Birkir stopped at probably the only gas station around to get himself a drink. He was nice enough to ask me if I wanted something, but I respectfully declined. I stayed inside the car while he entered the gas station. I was not too worried about Birkir because there was nobody around, and I was expecting him to return quickly. Inside the car, I turned on the radio. I was curious to know what kind of music people from Iceland listened to. I was disappointed because all the stations had very lousy signals. I was not aware of the time that had passed, since I was not paying attention. It was not until after thirty minutes that Birkir exited the station.

"Step out of the car," was the first thing Birkir said when he arrived.

"Walk with me." He continued, while I remained confused.

We walked to the end of the gas station, where one of the employees of the gas station was waiting with a small compact car. Birkir thanked the man before he handed him the keys to the car. I stared at the car in disbelief. The car was not in bad condition, but it was not as good as the last car. Birkir was all relaxed, enjoying the ice-cold soda he had purchased at the gas station.

"Why the change of cars?" I could not help but ask.

Birkir then turned to me to give me a slight smile.

"Have you forgotten your training?" Birkir replied.

For a second, I paused to see if something came to mind.

"The only way to defeat an enemy more powerful than you is through discretion. You must keep your enemies guessing at all times."

Once Birkir finished speaking, I remembered that exact moment when he taught us that lesson.

"Switching cars makes it harder for them to track me down," Birkir explained, just in case I did not understand.

On our way to the house, light rain began to fall. We arrived just before the rain started to come down hard. Birkir handed me a small towel to dry myself off a bit.

There was not much to do other than sit down and relax. Birkir was in the kitchen, pouring himself a nice glass of rosé wine. Without asking, he brought me a glass before sitting down facing me.

"You know? It's funny, I trained you for all those years, and I still don't know anything about you," Birkir said while taking a sip of wine.

"Is that a good thing?" I asked.

"It is a great thing. It means that you are discreet with your feelings," Birkir proudly told me.

"Have you spoken to Liam?"

"I have not seen him ever since."

"Liam was a good boy, but not as good as you."

"I would have to disagree," I replied.

"No, you are special, and the Society knows that," Birkir replied, while I leaned a bit backward.

"What will you do?" I asked, referring to his prospects.

"Enjoy my wine, and I ask a favor from you." Birkir took yet another sip from his almost empty wine glass.

"What would this favor be?"

"Call the Society, tell them your job is finished," Birkir said, looking firmly into my eyes.

"Is that all you need from me?" I asked, willing to help one of the most important men in my life.

"Yes."

Birkir left shortly after to take some time to meditate. I respected him and his time so much that I decided to exit the house to call the Canadian leaders' landline.

"Charles, do you have good news?" the Canadian leader asked.

"Of course, I have done what you asked of me."

"Did you confirm it was him?"

"Yes," I answered so that he would not become suspicious.

"Good. There will be a plane waiting for you tonight."

The Canadian leader hung up without saying goodbye.

I sat on the small bench outside Birkir's home to enjoy the beautiful scenery around me. My love for nature made me spend two hours outside the house. I went back inside to get myself a glass of cold water. Birkir was in the living room reading a book.

"I did what you asked me." I told him, clearly interrupting him.

"What did he say?" Birkir stopped reading his book to turn his attention to me.

"He congratulated me and told me that there will be a plane waiting for me tonight."

"I guess this is the end, then." Birkir said, not in a cheerful mood.

"For now, yes."

"As always, it has been a pleasure sharing time with you."

"Likewise, sir."

"I'll get someone to take you," were the last words he said before heading towards the telephone.

CHAPTER 6

UNUSUAL ENCOUNTER

Life has always been filled with surprises, especially for the members of the Society. Keeping the secret of who we are and what we do was key to the societies around the globe. Birkir meant everything to me; he taught me the ways of the Society and how someone should go live with discretion. Being discreet and polite was a big part of who we were. I had sworn to protect the Society at all costs. However, I was not very complacent with what the Society wanted me to do. I had been forced to spy on the man who trained me, and, from what I understood, that was not a common practice among the people of the Society.

One of Birkir's friends drove me to the gas station by the village, where another white van was waiting for me. I did not hesitate to get in the white van parked just a few feet away from the convenience store. The driver and I did not speak much, which was not bad news since it meant I did not have to make things up. The drive to the capital, Reykjavík, was a long one. Fortunately for me, I had the van all to myself. It finally came to a stop at the gate. Without any warning, the driver of the van rolled down my window. The Icelandic guard gave me a strange look before asking for my identification. I took my time since I was unsure if society members were allowed to do that. All the men had to do was read it from my hands to let the vehicle pass. My driver drove me straight to the hangar, where a private plane awaited me. The man opened the door and carried my luggage out of the trunk before I walked up the stairs and into the plane.

The inside of the plane was very similar to the one I had taken to get to Iceland. I sat in the first seat, just wanting to get home and relax. It did not take long for the plane to exit the hangar and take off from the runway. Once it was safe to remove the seat belt, one of the stewardesses approached me to ask if I wanted something to drink. I politely declined; all I wanted to do was to take a nap.

At the end of the flight, a moment of turbulence woke me up. The stewardess came and told me to fasten my seat belt, just in case things got a bit worse. I did as she said. It did not take long before the turbulence ended, and I was able to remove my seat belt. I lifted the window door, revealing the cloudy exterior that was most likely causing the turbulence.

The plane landed just a little over an hour later. Everything went smoothly, and I was ready to exit. The stewardess waved goodbye on my way out. I walked down the stairs, and the first person I saw was my father.

"How was the landing?" my father asked.

"Could not have been better."

My father picked me up from the airport. Due to society rules, we were unable to discuss anything concerning our jobs. Something was off, however. My dad was not heading to our house. He was heading to a wealthy neighborhood in the heart of Toronto. He stopped at a luxurious two-story house. At that precise moment, I was deeply confused. My father stepped out of the vehicle, and since I did not know what was going on, I decided to step out of the car.

I was confused by what I was seeing. Without saying a word, my father stepped out of the car. I decided to do the same.

"What do you think?" were the words of my father once I stepped out of the vehicle.

"I think the house is perfect, although it is unclear to me why you ask," I replied, while my father reached for the keys in his pockets.

"No. I cannot accept this," I said, not believing what I was witnessing.

"If you accepted to become a member, then you can surely accept this beautiful house."

I stared at him before turning my attention back to the house.

The interior of the home, while not expansive, perfectly suited my needs. As I moved through the space, my father remained by the kitchen, a hub of warmth and activity. The walls were adorned in a soothing light blue hue, creating an inviting ambiance. The interior design was particularly captivating, skillfully blending modern aesthetics with traditional decor, resulting in a harmonious atmosphere. Every element within the house complemented one another, reflecting an acute attention to detail. After completing my exploration, I made my way back to the eye-catching kitchen—a well-proportioned space where my father awaited my return.

"Final thoughts?" my father asked as I was walking towards him.

"It's perfect," I replied, even though I had something on my mind. "Why are you doing this?"

"The gift is not from me; it is from our leader," my father said.

"The Society believes you will be safer here."

"Safer?" I replied quickly, not knowing what he meant.

"The society has different objectives; we don't always know what they are. But you can be certain that they will make the right decision."

I acted like I understood, but in reality, I didn't.

"By the way, your mom still misses you; she is keen on preparing you a nice meal at least once a week."

I nodded while my dad walked away.

A month had elapsed, yet I still found it challenging to adjust to the weighty responsibility of being a member of the society. My daily existence was not unpleasant; rather, it was a significant departure from the routine I had maintained for the previous six years. I committed to exercising daily, as my role offered little in the way of physical activity. This regimen became essential, providing the equilibrium necessary to fulfill my obligations to the Society, particularly my primary duty of analyzing the origins of various attacks. The gravitas of my position was underscored by the fact that I controlled financial accounts linked to influential institutions. Fortunately, I was able to employ the calming techniques I had learned during my training with Birkir, which helped me navigate the pressures of my new role.

I had made a habit of meditating a few minutes before having my lunch. My efficiency came from taking my meditation sessions so seriously. That moment of pure peace was what I required to deal with the huge responsibility that I had, both at work and in life in general. Something disturbing used to happen from time to time. The ghost of Matt would suddenly appear while I was in meditation mode.

Something a little out of the usual happened when I

was exiting through the revolving doors of the building. I came across Jelena, the woman I had randomly met. From her facial expression, I could tell that she was more enthusiastic about seeing me than I was about seeing her.

"Charles! How are you?"

"I couldn't be better."

"Would you like to go for a walk?"

It was not what I wanted to do. However, I did not consider the possibility of denying her request because she had asked me in such a kind way. From my perspective, things were a bit awkward, since I was not allowed to reveal much about myself. I dominated the conversation until we ran into a street performer who was playing the trumpet. The performer was really talented; the look on her face was odd. I could not guess the motive for her strange expression. She took out her small wallet and tipped the man a ten-dollar bill before we kept walking.

"You enjoy music?" I genuinely asked.

"I enjoy art in general. It is a unique way in which we express who we are without fully revealing our true selves," Jelena replied.

This hit me very hard, even though I did not have much of an artistic background. This was the moment when my whole prospect of her changed. We kept walking until the end of the downtown area. We stood face-to-face with each other. Before we parted ways, I politely asked her if she would like to dine with me on one of the coming days. She immediately approved.

Back at the house, I turned on my gaming console and started playing a game I had purchased a while back. I did not like to do it because it took my focus away for the hours that I would play. However, I occasionally liked to enjoy my time off.

Upon completing my game, I indulged in a refreshing cold bath, which I found quite rejuvenating. The unique sound of water cascading into the tub was particularly enjoyable. Once the tub was filled, I turned off the tap and closed my eyes, entering a state of meditation. For me, meditation often feels like flipping a coin; the outcomes are unpredictable. However, this time felt distinct. The presence of a woman, with whom I was gradually developing feelings, abruptly occupied my thoughts. Keeping my eyes closed allowed me to better attune to her energy. While many may dismiss such experiences as ineffective, I believe they hold genuine significance, since every individual carries a unique essence that contributes to their mystique.

Fifteen minutes later, I opened my eyes before slowly rising out of the tub. Her energy was difficult to grasp. The only thing I got was that she was in deep pain. I checked my phone, which was lying on my bed. I put on a pair of pants and a shirt and headed outside the house.

My parents's house was relatively near mine. Once I arrived, I knocked and rang the bell a few times before my mother opened the door. She gave me a warm kiss on the cheek and told me to come in. My father was sitting at the table reading a magazine. He stopped once he saw me and greeted me with a hug and a few pats on the back. My mom came back with a delicious meat dish she had cooked. This was definitely her signature dish. I remembered when all our friends and family would come asking for the recipe. It was a secret that my mother would not give up, not even to my father. We had a nice evening; we shared countless memories and countless laughs with each other. It was time for dessert, and my mom had a surprise for both my dad and me. I struggled to hide the excitement about what my mom had to offer. I chuckled slightly at my dad, who replied similarly. She took quite a long time to put the large square pan in the middle of the table. It was a delicious cherry pie. The first bite was indescribable. The pie had a unique flavor that I absolutely enjoyed. My father did not stop complimenting how delicious the pie was. It was one of the most joyful moments that I can remember. Just when I thought the night was over, the doorbell chimed. My father and I looked at each other confused. My mother opened the door and let in my two cousins, whom she had lots of affection for. I did not have much of a bond with them; I barely knew them. However, judging by their playful nature, it was evident that they were two troublemakers.

My parents' house was just a short drive from mine, a comforting familiarity that welcomed me home. As I arrived, I knocked on the door and rang the bell a few times, and soon my mother swung it open with a bright smile. She greeted me with a warm kiss on the cheek and beckoned me inside. My father was at the table, lost in the pages of a magazine, but he quickly looked up when he heard my footsteps. A wide grin spread across his face as he stood to embrace me, offering a few hearty pats on the back that felt like a warm welcome.

A moment later, my mother emerged from the kitchen, proudly carrying a beautifully arranged plate of her signature meat dish. Its savory aroma filled the air, instantly bringing back memories of family gatherings where friends would plead for the recipe. I smiled at the thought; my mother was fiercely protective of that secret, never once revealing it, not even to my father, who would joke about it with mock exasperation.

As the evening unfolded, laughter and shared stories flowed freely around the table. We reminisced about our favorite moments, each memory punctuated by bursts of laughter that echoed against the walls. When it was time for dessert, my mother clapped her hands together in delight and revealed a surprise for both my dad and me. I could hardly hide my excitement, grinning at my father, who mirrored my anticipation.

After what felt like a delightful eternity, she finally set a large square pan at the center of the table, unveiling a cherry pie that glistened under the light. The first bite was pure bliss, a perfect blend of tart and sweet that made my taste buds dance. My father couldn't stop complimenting its delightful flavor, and in that instance, I knew this was one of those precious memories that would linger long after the last bite.

Just as I thought the night was coming to an end, the doorbell chimed, ringing through the warmth of our home. My father and I exchanged curious glances, and with a joyful flourish, my mother opened the door to welcome in my two cousins, whom she adored. Although I didn't know them well, their lively and playful energy made it clear they had a knack for stirring up mischief. With a hint of excitement, I realized that the evening was far from over; new adventures awaited us all.

My cousins were thrilled to see me and eager to engage in a quick game of chess. Although I had not played in quite some time, I was ready to embrace the challenge. As I began with the white pieces, I took on the responsibility of making the first move. The game remained closely contested until my eighty-ninth move. I carefully considered my options, aware of the precarious position I was in. Despite my low chances of victory and my growing fatigue, I unfortunately made a suboptimal move. My cousin, who preferred to avoid premature celebrations—a sentiment we both shared—waited until he recognized my defeat before exclaiming

"checkmate," which elicited a joyful laugh from me.

"Good game," I told him.

Moments later, I spotted my father out in the backyard. I sat on the chair next to him.

"Enjoying the view?"

He did not answer.

"You don't have to do it if you don't want to," my father said in a low tone. His statement caught me well off guard; I thought he was proud of me. I kept it cool.

"Dad, my decision was made a long time ago."

Both of us exchange the same look of agreement.

From a distance, we heard a flurry of bullets shattering the front window. I got on the ground immediately. My family inside would not stop screaming for help. Just a few feet away from me was my father, taking cover and analyzing what direction the bullets were coming from, just like I was. The moment was frightening; my family was in a great deal of danger. Luckily, the firing stopped. My father ran to the back storage room, knowing very well that the enemy was out of ammo. I hesitated to follow him, but I eventually did.

I entered the large shed, where the inner walls rotated, revealing a large screen with an advanced satellite system of our street. The technology was unlike anything that I had ever seen. My father worked out the system ten times better than I ever could. It was only a matter of minutes before he found out who the person shooting into our room was. Subsequently, he obtained footage from the residence, revealing that all individuals were unharmed, except for one of my cousins, who had sustained a gunshot wound to his right arm. The image of him screaming was painful to watch.

"Take care of him; I will terminate the shooter."

I nodded to my father, who was about to grab a semi-automatic shotgun he had hidden in a rectangular box.

The bullets once again penetrated the house at an incredibly fast speed. I cautiously counted each bullet and waited until the shooter ran out of bullets before carefully entering the house.

Responding swiftly to my mother's urgent cries for help, I hurried to the kitchen to retrieve the first aid kit. At that moment, I seemed to operate on instinct, unaware of the gravity of the situation unfolding around me. My mother and aunt were visibly distressed, their terrified screams resonating through the air. Meanwhile, my cousin lay injured, having sustained a gunshot wound that resulted in substantial blood loss.

"Relax, he will be fine," I asked my mother to calm the situation. However, the moment was so dreadful that she was unable to do as I asked.

I took a deep breath to enhance my focus, consciously tuning out the distressing sounds of my aunt's cries and my mother's desperate sobs. I examined the wound to assess the extent of the bullet's penetration. Fortunately, it had not inflicted damage to any major arteries.

Rapidly, I checked the first aid kit and selected the scalpel, and before taking it out of its packaging, my aunt held my hand. Which basically meant to cautiously think before taking action.

"Everything will be fine, I promise," I confidently told her.

As I assessed the wound, I noted the bullet's trajectory and depth of penetration. With careful precision, I prepared to manage the injury. After ensuring that the area was adequately cleaned and sterilized, I made an incision to remove any debris and damaged tissue surrounding the entry point. I then applied direct pressure to stop the bleeding while suturing the wound methodically to promote healing. Luckily, the bullet had not damaged any major arteries, which allowed for a more straightforward surgical intervention.

My father arrived a few minutes later; I was sitting by myself at the dining room table.

"How is the boy?" he asked when he saw me.

"He is fine; I managed to stitch him up. Still, I believe he should be taken to the hospital." He nodded before grabbing a cold beer from the fridge. He placed the beer on the table furiously.

"Did you catch him?" I asked, even though I knew that he was unhappy.

He took a sip before replying, "He was toying with

us."

"What do you mean?" I asked, confused. He finished the beer before replying. "Both you and I need to get out of our places," my father said with a concerned look on his face.

"Do they know where I live?" I asked.

"Yes," my father quickly replied.

"Where shall I go then?" I asked.

"Somewhere difficult to locate," replied my father before leaving the table, with a cold look in his eyes.

I went back to the house, even though my father told me not to; I had to pick up all the classified stuff before leaving the place for good. Flashbacks came to me while I was driving on the busy Canadian highway. Bad daydreams that had been haunting me since the training. Eventually, I snapped out of it, although not fully; it was enough for me to focus on what I was going to do. Things got worse when traffic started to intensify, and I was suddenly going at ten miles per hour. It was unexpectedly helpful; it was the time when I figured out where I was going to be staying. I turned the music on the radio up, not knowing when the traffic jam would end.

The traffic finally cleared after approximately fifty minutes, allowing me to navigate the highway with a sense of urgency. As I exited, I found myself in a familiar yet desolate location, where the remnants of the past remained largely undisturbed. A wave of nostalgia washed over me upon sight of the wooden cabin where I had spent some of the most formative years of my life. This was the only place I had come to know intimately. As I retrieved my belongings from the trunk of my car, an inexplicable hesitation prevented me from entering the house.

Entering the house was like a trip down memory lane. I put my things at the front to take in the energy of the place. I served myself a glass of water before sitting on the seat by the fireplace. Time had passed, and I had not even noticed it. I sat there for about forty-five minutes, then I went upstairs. The furniture in the room was entirely different. After checking the upstairs area, I headed back down to sleep on the couch.

As always, the extraordinary view caught my attention. I stood by the front door with a nice tea mug in hand. It was early, so I had more than enough time to prepare for work. I decided to sit outside where the pile of tree logs used to be. A little over half an hour later, I started my car and left the cabin.

I was once more at the cybersecurity building. Walking in, I was cautious, thinking maybe someone here could be watching me. My office was clean and organized; the only difference was a note left on the desk saying that there would be a meeting at four o'clock. I turned on my computer and got to work on the tasks that were still pending. The days when I could work quickly and effectively were always a good sign for me. Since I was not hungry, I decided to do a bit more research on the person who had tried to kill my family.

Before leaving my parents, I had taken one of the bullets that had penetrated the house. I opened an incognito web browser to dig for some information. I had to search thoroughly to get a trace of the bullet. Fortunately for me, I had a natural gift for utilizing computer systems. After about two hours, I had managed to find every single piece of information I needed about the bullet. I was convinced that the people who had attacked us were most likely members of a different society. The weapons were bought in Ireland from a classified seller. That person had later bought a ticket to Toronto under a name that did not exist. After getting deeper into the subject, I ran into a terrifying revelation: the man was working under a false identity at a building not too far from where I was.

Without a pinch of hesitation, I walked towards the massive building where the supposed shooter was working. People were constantly entering and exiting the building. A man wearing a safety vest walked past me. I followed him and offered him a good amount of money in exchange for his helmet, white clipboard, and the vest. The man did not think twice and accepted what I had just proposed to him.

The outfit was the ticket inside. I stopped at the main reception and said I had been called in to check the electrical system. The receptionist did not even bother to verify who I was. The building was as nice as the place that I was working at. I followed the exit signs, which led me to the stairs, strangely not in the same modern conditions as the interior halls. I analyzed all the floors carefully, intending to find some sort of evidence. There was little to no light in some spots, which made me turn on the flashlight on my phone. I managed to look at all the steps on the floors and check where each of the exit doors led to. I had done everything I could, and I was ready to leave. Someone just entered the stairs through the ground level; I was not fazed. That was until I crossed paths with the man.

He intentionally kicked me from behind, knocking me down to the floor. I recovered quickly, knowing that my life could very well be in danger. The man pulled out a pocket-knife and started moving it like a nunchuck. I was ready for this moment. The man tried to cut me several times, but he missed terribly. I managed to kick him a few times in his leg. He was still rock solid. We kept fighting it off through the stairs. I managed to disarm him, but it didn't turn out to be a good idea because that only made him angrier than he already was. He pushed me against the wall and started punching me, which caused me to lose my stamina. Eventually, I was able to escape and hit him on the neck. The blow was so hard that he fell to the floor immediately. I was afraid that he would try to hurt me once more, so I kicked him numerous times in the face. The fight was over, and the man was most likely dead. I sat just a few feet below him to catch my breath. That was the first time that I had killed someone. The scariest part about it was the empty feeling that I had inside, almost as if it were the right thing to do, even though I had just committed a crime. I got up immediately, not wanting to spend any more time next to a dead body. I took the man's phone so I could check it when my mind was clear.

With an energy drink in my hand, I returned to my office. I made sure that the blinds were closed to fully relax. It was not the most ideal thing for me to do, but I needed to attend an important meeting.

The conference room was almost empty by the time I arrived. This was both good and bad for me. People were socializing, having friendly conversations. But I was not in the mood to join in. Luckily, the meeting began shortly after. An elderly man with graying hair from a Hungarian tech company commenced his presentation. The presentation was about a new system they wanted to implement on our software. Everything went well, especially since the meeting ended a little over an hour.

My workday was over; it was time to unwind from a very stressful day. I tried to turn on the TV, but there was no signal. I went outside to try to fix the old antenna. Once there, I removed all the dirt and leaves that could have been interfering with the signal. The wind started to blow intensely at me. I stopped because it was becoming a bit challenging. Something moved on the ground when I turned around. I caught a glimpse of the silhouette of a human. I tried to take a closer look to identify the person, but unfortunately, they were gone by then. On my way back to the house, I stared at the bushes, believing that someone may be hiding. There was no one, however, which was a little worrying because I thought I was seeing things that were not present. I went back inside, where I turned on the TV to watch a game show.

Without realizing, I had fallen asleep. The sound of a bell woke me up. I looked everywhere to see where the noise was coming from. It was just the end of the game show. I went straight to the fridge to get a nice cold water bottle.

Something hit me all of a sudden, which was the fact that I was not going to keep the promise that I made with Jelena. The situation that my family and I were in was very puzzling. I sent her a quick text, telling her that I deeply apologized for not being able to keep my word. She replied instantly, telling me not to worry about it and suggesting we reschedule it for another day. That problem was solved, but I was not satisfied with my decision.

I put my phone to the side and began my investigation, on the phone, of the man who tried to kill me earlier. I was able to access it in no time. The only issue was that all the information had been deleted. This made it harder, but not impossible, to track the man's history. I went back to the fridge to grab a club soda to help me put the hard work in. I spent the whole night trying, but sadly, I failed to get any further.

It was midnight, and I was exhausted from being in front of a computer all day. The weather was perfect to sit outside on the old rocking chair on the front porch of the house. The wind blew slowly towards me. It was quiet, except for all the wildlife making strange noises once the night hit. I was beginning to fall asleep, so I decided to go inside the cabin.

My worst fears suddenly came true. An unknown man held me at gunpoint.

"Sit," he said, directing his gun toward the sofa.

I walked to the sofa with no intention of trying to harm him. Something that caught my attention was the fact that if he wanted to kill me already, then he would have already done so. Without any concerns as to what the consequences were, maybe I sat on the couch and looked right into his gun without making any eye contact with him.

I figured that if he had wanted to, he would have killed me by then. I sat and looked right into his gun as if it were a camera.

"Who are you?" asked the man, pointing his gun at my head.

"My name is Charles, and I don't want any problems," I told him in a relaxed manner.

"Prove that you are who you say you are," demanded the man.

"I need to get my wallet, if you don't mind," I said

while trying to figure out why this man looked so familiar.

"Get up," said the man while still holding me at gun-point.

As I was walking, I was trying to figure out a way to disarm him, but the distance was too long for me to make a move. I got my wallet from the kitchen counter; the men told me to stop once I turned around. He swiftly took the wallet from my hands.

"You really are him," the man said, in a very surprised tone.

I slowly turned, thinking the situation had calmed down.

"Do you know who I am?" the man asked.

He looked familiar, but I did not have the slightest clue who he was.

"No," I replied a few moments later. He looked at me.

"I am the person who trained with you in this exact location," he said.

The deep respect we had for each other was deeply highlighted when we gave each other a warm hug, happy to have met in the place that meant everything to us.

Moments later, we were sitting in the kitchen, discussing what we had been up to. Even though we were enjoying each other's company, we had to get down to business.

"What are you doing here?" I wanted to know why our paths had crossed at the same place we met.

"Orders from the society. What about you? Why are

you here?" Liam asked me.

"Someone tried to murder my family." I said, with a concerned yet saddened voice tone.

Liam looked at me seriously.

"Your family will be safe, and whatever is going on, we will get to the bottom of it."

I looked at him while nodding in agreement.

After our chat, I went to the top floor of the house to arrange one of the rooms for him.

"Your room is ready," I told Liam when I went back downstairs.

Liam's attention shifted from the TV to me.

"Thanks, but I am fine where I am. You take the room upstairs for strategic purposes," Liam said very firmly. I went on with it because Liam was a bit more experienced than me.

I woke up fairly early the next morning, not in the mood to go to work. Once I got up, I did not hesitate to change into my work clothes. It was around 6:29, so I walked very quietly downstairs, not wanting to wake Liam up. However, the sofa where he was supposed to be sleeping was empty. I stepped outside, knowing that he was most likely to be sitting on the porch of the house. There he was, on the white rocking chair. He immediately turned around.

"Charles, please, accompany me."

I did as he asked and sat on the wooden chair next to

him.

"I still remember when we trained together," Liam said proudly.

"As do I. You were the confidence boost I needed to get me through the training," I told him.

"Do you have any information on our enemies?" Liam asked, clearly meaning business.

"No, I tried to access the phone of the man who tried to kill me yesterday, but he had already deleted everything."

Liam took a brief pause to admire the beautiful blue bird on top of the tree.

"Have you been speaking to anyone outside your job?" Liam asked.

"I have," I admitted shamefully, answering his question. He turned around.

"Who?"

"A woman I randomly met." Liam took a deep breath. I knew this was against what the Society wanted.

"Who is the woman?" Liam tensely asked.

"She is an employee of a nearby office."

"Is that all you know about her?"

I could only nod.

"Find out more about her; she could be working with the NEU."

He then got up from his chair and gave me a nice, warm pat on my leg. The sun was slowly beginning to rise, so I stayed out on the front porch a bit longer. Sunrise was my favorite part of the morning; it symbolized a chance to become better than I was yesterday.

Clouds were slowly moving near the sun. I got in my car with a laptop bag and a bottle of orange juice. I really was not feeling like working that day, but I drove to my workplace nevertheless. Once in the office, I arranged my things before turning on my computer to check what the task for the day was. My inbox showed two emails with instructions for the day. By the first hour, I had already finished the task that the company had sent me. It was now time for the important research: finding out more about Jelena. I began the search directly at CSN, a society network made for members of Canada. I managed to find her last name, Kohler, which I knew to be German. For a significant number of hours, I searched for information about the woman but didn't find any more significant information. This was a clear red flag.

I left the building to walk directly to where Jelena worked. There were not many people at the time, so I had to find a spot where she would not recognize me. Eventually, I found a table near a tree where she would not be able to see me. From there, I began to do further research on her. I checked my watch and saw that it was seven minutes to five o'clock when her shift ended. I turned my phone off to fully focus on her. Ten minutes later, all the workers had left the place. I was ready to leave until someone scared me from behind. I turned around, ready for war.

But it was only Jelena. I smiled at her, not wanting her to become suspicious.

"How did you know it was me?" I asked her.

She laughed and answered, "I saw you from my office, silly."

I was so upset by my poor decision-making, but I played it off because I had bigger plans.

She sat down, and we both began to mention our work lives and how stressful they could be from time to time. I had to open myself up to try to squeeze any piece of information out of her.

"So, where are you from?" She had no issues revealing her true German and Russian heritage. Many things came to my mind at that certain point.

"What about you?" Jelena asked genuinely.

"I'm from here," I answered quickly. The conversation ended when it started raining heavily, so we took shelter in a nearby café. I started to loosen up, being a bit naive about the bigger picture. We both ordered an iced coffee and sat in the booth at the end of the coffee shop. The place began to get busier by the minute. I got a call from my father shortly after. For some reason, it did not urge me. Jelena was special to me. I had no idea how to maneuver through the difficult situation I had in my hands. The rain stopped after a few minutes. We decided to leave the place because it was quite crowded by then.

I chose to accompany Jelena to her car; however, an

unexpected incident interrupted our departure when we heard an explosion emanating from the building where I work. Both Jelena and I were momentarily taken aback. Without hesitation, I departed from her side and sprinted toward the site of the explosion.

The sight inside could be compared to a scene from a movie. People were running like wild animals trying to exit the building. The alarm wouldn't stop ringing. I ran to the stairs. Everyone was coming down except me. On my way up, I ran into my boss.

"What in the world do you think you are doing?"

I ignored him and continued running upstairs. I stopped at the sixteenth floor, where my office was. The floor was undamaged. I walked towards my office door to find it locked. This was weird, since I never lock the door. A slow clapping sound from behind caught my attention.

I turned around, only to see a man with a black and gold mask standing next to two men with white and black masks.

"Just how I wanted to see you!" the man with the black and gold mask said.

"So you really think you are going to kill one of my men and get away with it?"

I looked straight into the man's eyes, without an ounce of fear in my body.

"I don't know about you, but for me, it is just business," I replied.

"Well, then it seems we are going to get along," the man said sarcastically.

"I find that highly unlikely."

"Then you would be disloyal to your society, but I believe you are not among the most loyal of men."

I looked at him without replying.

"Your society has something that is mine."

"And what is that?"

"Three of our men were hunted like dogs by your people. Today they are not half what they once were, but those men, just like you, have families waiting for them."

"Consider this a warning: there will be war. If you do not follow our rules, you, along with your men, will lose everything."

The leader signaled his men to leave. I sat there waiting for them to disappear.

I exited through the stairs shortly after. On my way down, I ran into a firefighter who advised I should exit the building as soon as possible.

Many journalists were already gathered outside the building and ran towards me once they saw me exiting. I did not answer a single question and managed to block all the unwanted attention from the journalist until I reached my car.

The drive home from the office made me reflect on how hard and complicated being a man of importance could be. Luckily, I arrived safely at my house. Liam wasn't home yet, which was good because I wanted to relax in the shower before I could explain things to him. The sound of the water coming down the faucet reminded me of the waterfalls from Iceland. Just a few seconds later, I got my towel and dried myself off. I put on some dry clothes before heading down the stairs.

I wanted a drink and mixed some cranberry juice with a bit of vodka. Since I wanted to clear my mind of things, I sat at the dining table, where I would simply enjoy my drink. The temperature outside was lovely; therefore, I decided to head out to enjoy the weather. The wind was cool, and the great outdoors was fairly calm, except for an owl, which I could only distinguish due to his vibrant orange eyes.

I looked up at the night sky, trying to figure out the constellations. Something odd happened. An envelope dropped from above, just a few feet away from where I was standing. I looked around cautiously before even thinking of picking it up. I wanted to know what it contained. However, my instincts told me to take a different route.

I returned to the cabin, made my way upstairs, and approached the wardrobe. Although I had no specific plans to go out, I changed into more casual attire to ensure I'd be comfortable should anything unexpected occur.

I grabbed my handgun along with my tactical flashlight from my night table. I went straight to the air conditioning unit and entered a PIN on the thermostat. The unit slid to the left, revealing a secret underground walkway. I kept a blank face, but I was not content with the fact that I had forgotten to get my landmine detector. Swiftly but discreetly, I went back upstairs to grab the device from the other night table. Fully equipped, I made my way underground.

The wooden stairs made an unbearable noise that I absolutely hated. I continued on my way on the dark underground path. Even though I was not frightened, walking in the darkness was quite the experience. I cautiously checked the rough tile floors with my mine detector. The device was one of a kind; its range extended from top to bottom. This helped me determine whether it was safe to set another foot in front. I walked past different doors without any issue; everything seemed ok. I went back to the house and locked the passage from the thermostat. My task was finished; it was now time for me to head out. I stepped out carefully, knowing that there could be somebody watching, and I picked up the envelope. There was a note saying, "Remember what we spoke about."

Liam came as I was reading the note.

"What is it?" he asked.

I did not reply but handed him the note.

"Do you know who it is from?"

"My guess is that it comes from the man I met earlier at work."

Liam looked at me, deeply concerned.

"What man?"

"The man who caused the explosion at my job. He was wearing a black and gold mask. He wants our society to release their people."

Speechless, Liam sat on the sofa.

"Who are the people they want us to release?"

"Wealthy communist men who have access to a network a network of higly dangerous profesionals across different fields of work."

"They're just like us, then."

"Yes, only more sinister and less forgiving."

Liam stood up to release his stress.

"It took us years to catch them; they cost the lives of many of our men," Liam made this statement concerned about the possible consequences.

"Get some rest; I will find a way to sort things out," he added before I headed to my room.

CHAPTER 7

UNEXPECTEAD JOURNEY

Even though it had been a tough couple of days, I was able to get six hours of sleep, enough for me to re-charge and tackle the obstacles of the next day. I woke up just in time to follow my usual routine before work. The loud noise coming from downstairs made me wonder what was going on. I reached the first floor, where Liam was packing all the objects in the house into boxes. He was fully focused, so he did not bother to look at me until I walked closer.

"Mind giving me a hand?" Liam asked while putting the ceramic plates into the box.

"What is this all about?"

He paused for a moment before continuing with his

work.

"This place has been put to good use."

I stared into his eyes, confused, not knowing what he was trying to tell me. Luckily, he noticed it.

"We can't leave any traces, Charles. What makes us dangerous is that hardly any people know who we are. Remember that differences in opinions cause revolution, and revolutions cause chaos," Liam told me, intending to educate me. He continued packing, slowly increasing the pace. For an hour and a half, we worked non-stop.

Finally, we finished packing all the items in the house. It was now time to pack my things and head out. Leaving this place for good was not a good feeling at all. I became the man who I was thanks to this place; yes, there were difficult moments, but they were essential in helping me grow. I got dressed up and headed out of the house, possibly for one last time. Liam was already outside the house, waiting by the car.

"Take a closer look, Charles."

I turned around to take one last look at the house. I began to get those strange flashbacks I used to get, but it did not matter because these were filled with great memories.

"I need you to help me do one more thing. Liam stood to one side, revealing multiple gasoline tanks. I was apathetic to the situation, but deep down it felt painful. An intelligent Liam picked up the sad energy that I was subconsciously transmitting.

"Trust me, this is as hard for me as it is for you. However, we have a duty."

Liam gave me a pat on the shoulder before beginning to pour the gasoline around the area. Once again, I helped him. I poured the gasoline all around the cabin. Liam pulled out a matchbox from his pocket. Without hesitation, he threw the match into the gasoline path we had made just a few feet away from the front porch of the house. The fire slid slowly into the house, and once it hit the house, the fire began to rise into the air. The fire made the surroundings warmer. I checked my watch; I was already late for work.

I turned to Liam and said, "Sorry, but I have to go."

Liam immediately turned to me and asked, "Go where?"

I was in a rush, and I really did not have much time to react.

"Your job today is not at the office; it is to follow my lead."

Liam's firm statement left me thinking. All the thoughts came to an end when he took out the fire extinguishers from his car. He handed me one of them before putting out the fire himself. I took a brief pause before assisting him.

It was the first time that I had used a fire extinguisher. However, I got the hang of it. Putting out the fire was much harder than causing it. For me, it was a hidden sign of the importance of keeping the peace. After a very exhausting forty-five minutes, we were done. Shortly after taking a break, we picked up all the debris from the ground. Liam did not say a word to me because he wanted to finish as quickly as possible. I, on the other hand, was enjoying the job; it was satisfying to finally let go of the past. This gave me a sense of calm that I had not yet experienced. I began to sweat a bit, so I took out my long-sleeve shirt to cool myself down. After four long hours, we had completed the job; all the debris was piled up in one place. Liam and I stood next to each other; he was looking at the accumulated debris we had piled up, while I was looking at my surroundings. He then turned to me.

"Follow me, we still have a long journey ahead," he said.

I followed Liam with my car. This time we drove south. He was driving at a steady pace, most likely because he did not want to lose me. He took an exit two hours into our journey, which led us to a beautiful small town. Liam stopped at an empty bar. The place looked quite nice from the outside. I turned off the instrumental music on the radio before hopping out of the car.

The interior exuded a pristine cleanliness, gleaming surfaces reflecting the soft glow of overhead lights. Every item was meticulously arranged, almost as if curated for a display, from the neatly stacked magazines on the coffee table to the perfectly aligned chairs around the booths.

The walls told a vibrant story, adorned with an eclectic collection of photographs that captured moments from the 1950s through the 1980s, each framed image a window into a bygone era, evoking nostalgia with their sepia tones and candid smiles.

"What do you think?" Liam asked while looking at the glossy menu.

Something caught my attention: there was no one at the bar. I looked at Liam, but he did not look back at me. My senses told me something was wrong, but I did not know Liam's past with this particular place.

Shortly after, an old man with a well-groomed, white beard approached the table.

"It is my friend's first time, so please, bring us something for the occasion."

Liam demanded this without even giving the waiter a chance to speak. The old man left without even saying thank you. I looked at Liam, who gave me a strange look back.

"You should learn to trust me a bit more," Liam said, slightly smirking.

We began to talk about the few inconveniences of our trip. The old man brought us two glasses of water, along with two cups of tea. Liam thanked the man before he left. I took a sip of the ice-cold water. At the same moment that I put my glass of water down, the curtains began to come down. The interior became dark all of a sudden. I, intuitively, looked around to get a more profound understanding of what was happening. I stared into Liam's cold eyes. His attention was directed to the rest of the coffee shop. I did not want to, but I had to ask him.

"What is going on?"

"Please, Charles, remain patient," was his simple reply.

Members of the society were cautious about where and when they would discuss things despite being in what we called a mute zone, especially in times when the enemy roamed around our country. The old man, who was our server, placed aluminum antennas just to make sure nobody would listen to us.

Shortly after, two Canadian members walked inside. Liam and I stood up, showing respect to our fellow members. All four of us exchanged handshakes before taking our seats. The members did not waste time asking us what had happened.

I began my story by telling them everything from the beginning. They were not fazed by anything I told them. However, something did worry them. The fact that I had been interacting with Jelena was something that they found concerning. It was not the fact that I was talking to a woman that made them mad, but the way she introduced herself to me. Jelena had always been polite and respectful. However, everything that Jelena had done was quite suspicious to them. They left shortly after, happy that I had told them all the details of what had occurred.

The elderly man waited for the Canadian members to leave to put away the antennas and put down the blind. The waiter, then, came on to our table to ask if we wanted something for the road. It was safe to say that both Liam and I were thankful for his great service; however, neither of us wanted to order food to go. The waiter wished us well before informing us that we did not have to pay for the tea. Nevertheless, Liam did not hesitate to give the man a tip for his good service.

We merged onto the highway, the familiar stretch of asphalt stretching out before us like a ribbon of opportunity. The day had started off promising; the sun bathed the highway in a warm glow, and everything seemed fine. However, our serenity was abruptly shattered when we encountered a protest that had erupted on the roadside, causing a massive traffic jam that seemed to stretch endlessly in both directions.

Frustration began to creep in as the standstill grew more pronounced. I leaned back in my seat and took a deep breath, inhaling all the air I could, in an attempt to calm the anxious fluttering in my chest. My fingers tapped nervously on the steering wheel as I turned on the radio, desperate to hear news about the situation unfolding ahead. As I flipped through the stations, I became increasingly disappointed—none of them were reporting on the protest or explaining what had transpired. The silence of the airwaves only heightens my sense of unease.

To quiet my racing thoughts, I settled on some sooth-ing instrumental music, letting the gentle melodies wrap around me like a comforting blanket. Nevertheless, after twenty long minutes of unmoving cars and frustrated honks echoing around us, it became painfully clear that we hadn't made any progress. My heart sank a little as I no-ticed that Liam was nowhere to be seen in the other car; the absence of his reassuring presence was beginning to gnaw at my mind. Why wasn't he here with me? An unset-tling feeling settled deep within me, combining with the tension of the stalled traffic, as I glanced into the rearview mirror, hoping to catch a glimpse of the familiar silhouette of his vehicle.

I got out of the car, even though it was not what I wanted to do. People were infuriated at the fact that a silly protest had blocked them from reaching their destination. The protest was not civil at all; it was very crude. People with black skull masks were throwing rocks and smoke gre-nades towards random civilians. I was able to disregard all the violence and continue on with my objective, which was to find Liam's car. I walked for about a mile unsuccessfully. All of a sudden, I became anxious. The horrible flashbacks kicked in. I was beginning to feel more and more disorient-ed by the minute. I stood still for around five minutes while putting my hand on my forehead. The short headache had suddenly gone away, but the protest had intensified. Once more, I began to search for Liam's car, but after walking endlessly in circles, I was unable to locate it.

At that moment, I was not particularly concerned; I thought he might have exited the highway without telling me. I walked all the way to the front, where a man stood with a megaphone speaking about the corruption of the government. I did not pay too much attention because the issue did not concern me.

A whirring helicopter suddenly descended from the sky, its powerful spotlight cutting through the chaos like a knife, illuminating the figure of the man with the megaphone as if he were the center of a dark stage. Meanwhile, heavily armed police officers, clad in tactical gear that gleamed ominously in the harsh light, began to storm the scene with an intimidating show of force. The air crackled with tension as the police, faced with an unruly crowd that showed no signs of yielding, felt they had no choice but to resort to brutal enforcement tactics against the protestors, who stood their ground defiantly.

Instantly, what had started as a demonstration of voices and passion descended into a horrifying bloodbath, the sounds of sirens and shouts mingling with the unmistakable thud of violence erupting amid shattering ideals. The protestors, resolute in their beliefs, continued to defy the law, fully aware of the grim repercussions that awaited them, yet unwilling to back down.

My heart raced as I felt the overwhelming urge to retreat to the safety of the car, to escape the wickedness and turmoil unfolding around me like a nightmarish landscape. But a more pressing concern held me captive; I couldn't leave without knowing the whereabouts of Liam's car. As if a sixth sense guided me amid the chaos, I suddenly spotted his vehicle trapped in the fray, a beacon of familiarity in the madness. Yet, a wave of dread washed over me when I realized that Liam himself was nowhere to be found. Anxiety was knotted in my stomach as I approached his car, only to see his phone lying abandoned on the floor of the driver's seat, a lifeline to his intended destination amidst all this confusion. I quickly grabbed it, hoping that it might hold the key to locating him and uncovering where he had gone in the midst of this unfolding chaos.

I returned to my car to put all the pieces together. However, it was difficult to actually do so. It took about two hours to clear the protestors off the highway. I thought about telling the police about Liam, but I didn't do it out of respect for Liam and the Society. I passed by multiple blinding blue lights. The road was still packed. I drove for a few more hours before I eventually decided to exit towards a town I did not know.

At the precise moment I entered the small town, it began to rain. Just one more inconvenient thing that was happening on this crazy day. Mother Nature was uncontrollable; all I could do was continue trying to find a place where I could stay. A small neon sign gave me huge satisfaction at the moment. I entered the parking lot of the modest hotel. The rain was still heavy. However, it did not stop me from stepping out of the car with my backpack, which I kept on the passenger seat.

Two glass doors smoothly parted in opposite directions, unveiling a small yet inviting lobby that radiated warmth and comfort. The air was filled with a faint, soothing scent of polished wood and fresh linen. Behind the polished front desk, a receptionist stood, her demeanor professional but approachable. As I stepped into the lobby, water dripped incessantly from my clothes, pooling around my feet, highlighting my disheveled appearance. Sensing my presence, she turned to me, her eyes widening slightly as a flicker of surprise crossed her face, a mix of curiosity and concern playing across her features. At that moment, however, I was too exhausted and overwhelmed by the tumultuous day to register her reaction. All I cared about was securing a room where I could wash away the remnants of the day—a hot shower to soothe my weary body was all I desired. Despite my bedraggled state, the receptionist's gentle demeanor put me at ease, and she promptly assisted me with a smile, guiding me through the process with efficiency and kindness. Gratefully, I made my way to the elevator, the soft hum of the machinery welcoming me as the doors slid shut. Before long, I arrived at the fourth floor, where my room awaited, a sanctuary from the chaos I had just escaped.

After a strange day, I was able to fully relax. Like always, I let the water run down through my skin. The water was as warm as it could be. I finished quickly because I wanted to go to sleep. I got out and put on a fresh robe, turned off the night light, and went directly to sleep.

The next morning, I woke up around ten in the morning. Not to my surprise, I overslept a bit. Another strange thing would occur: a man whom I did not know was sitting on the armchair in my room.

"Do you know why I'm here?"

I shook my head. The man remained stone-cold.

"Your friend has been taken hostage by the society we are yet to identify. We are not sure, but we believe it is linked with the deal the NEU wants you to make."

Upon hearing the news, I was taken aback, momentarily at a loss for words as my thoughts centered solely on the life of my dear friend Liam. Meanwhile, the man rose confidently from his chair.

"Our issues will be resolved; they always are," he stated. The man gave me a note with an address. "Meet me at this location."

I immediately lay back on my bed, not understanding anything that was going on. All I knew was that the people I loved were in danger because of the Society. This made me feel guilty about myself. I got up from the comfortable bed and changed into more casual clothes.

The lobby of the hotel was empty. I stopped at the breakfast area to grab an orange juice and a bowl of cereal before heading out. The weather that morning had nothing to do with last night's rainy weather. The sun was out, and it was beautiful. Even though the sun was shining bright, the wind breeze made the temperature pleasant. I opened the driver's door of my car and took out the note the man had given me and put the address on my phone. I took a sip of the ice-cold orange juice before starting the car. It was around eleven o'clock, which was perfect for me; everyone would be at work, which meant little to no traffic. The road was clear, and that was my excuse to drive above the speed limit. I arrived fairly quickly at my destination, which was at the border between the US and Canada.

I was pulled over by an American border patrol officer, his expression dark and scrutinizing as he approached my vehicle to request my passport. The man's piercing gaze held an unsettling intensity, and I sensed that displeasing him further could lead to complications I wanted to avoid. With a nod of compliance, I quickly handed him my passport, the paper somehow feeling heavier in that charged moment. The officer took his time, meticulously examining the document as if it contained secrets that needed uncovering. To pass the tense silence, I attempted to turn on the radio, hoping for some distraction, but only a crackle and intermittent static greeted me; I quickly decided to turn it off again.

After what felt like an eternity, the officer finally returned, my passport gripped tightly in his hand, his demeanor far from welcoming. "Step out of the vehicle," he commanded, his tone semi-rude and authoritative. I did not hesitate; the heightened atmosphere demanded compliance. I exited the car and positioned myself a few feet away, my pulse steady despite the unease that tinged the air. There was little to worry about aside from the concealed gun I had stashed in a hidden compartment, a precaution I had taken seriously.

I got stopped by an American border patrol. For some reason, the man gave me an ill look while asking for my passport. Not wanting to displease the man any more than he seemed, I quickly handed him my passport. The border patrolman took his time. I turned on the radio, but it was not working properly, so I turned it back off. The patrolman returned thirty minutes later with my passport in his hand. He asked me to step out of the vehicle in a semi-rude way. I did not hesitate to do what he asked of me. I got out of the car and stood a few feet away from him. There was nothing to worry about, apart from my gun, which I concealed in a hidden spot. The patrol took its sweet time checking my car. He then kindly asked me to open the trunk. I opened it without hesitation; it was fully empty, making it a quick procedure for the patrol.

"You are good to go," the patrol said.

I happily got back in the car and continued my journey. It was a new experience for me; I had never been to the US. Nothing had changed, yet everything felt different.

I was extremely astonished to see the number of cars that drove on the highway. I reached for my phone, which was in the cupholder next to me. While multitasking, which is not a good thing to do while driving, I checked my phone to see how much time I had left to reach my destination. I drove straight for one more hour before stopping at a local gas station. The exterior of the station was similar to the ones back in Canada; the only difference was that the people dressed a bit differently, and the interior had various snacks that the ones in Canada did not have.

Nevertheless, I entered the gas station, where many people were in a line. The woman at the cash register was quite slow. I did not get annoyed, but the rest of the people who were in line did; in fact, they started complaining about the poor service. The manager of the gas station was forced to open another register to quiet down the rowdy customers. Luckily, the line moved up quickly; it was my turn, and to my odd luck, the slow woman was the one that would take care of me. As I was going to tell her my tank number, the manager stopped what he was doing to take care of my order. I gave him my twenty-dollar bill, and he immediately gave me my receipt.

Returning to my car, I managed to fill the tank to only a quarter of its capacity, a meager amount that would have to suffice for the journey ahead to the bustling heart of New York City. As I drove, anticipation bubbled within me. The city loomed ahead, more majestic than I had ever dared to imagine. The skyscrapers, colossal and awe-in-spiring, seemed to pierce the heavens, their glossy surfaces reflecting the muted glow of the evening sun, making it nearly impossible for me to glimpse their towering roofs. I often found myself craning my neck as I navigated the streets, a habit I picked up to gauge just how high they reached.

The traffic was unyielding, a serpentine flow of yellow taxis weaving through the landscape like a flock of bright canaries. While the vibrant energy of the city enveloped me in a spell of wonder, I forced myself to focus; I was merely blocks away from my destination. With each turn I took, anticipation surged within me until finally, I spotted the building. It stood proudly, not as towering as its neigh-bors, but possessing a unique design that set it apart, a fu-sion of modern aesthetics and whimsical charm.

Now that I had arrived, a flicker of relief washed over me, but my mission wasn't complete—I needed to find a place to park. As I scoured the streets, fortune smiled upon me; I discovered a vacant spot just a few feet from the entrance. The car lot felt inviting, its sparse population of vehicles mirroring the calm before the impending hustle of twilight. With the sun dipping lower in the sky, casting long shadows on the pavement, I realized I had arrived a few precious minutes early—time enough to collect my thoughts before plunging into the city's vibrant embrace.

As I stepped into the building, a well-dressed porter

in a crisp, tailored uniform gracefully opened the door for me, the rich fabric of his suit glimmering under the soft glow of the interior lights. The entrance was welcoming yet modest in size; it wasn't cramped, but in comparison to the grandiose lobbies of other establishments I had visited, it felt almost intimate. Smooth marble floors reflected the soft ambient lighting, while textures of warm woods and subtle artwork added character to the space.

My gaze was drawn to a striking ornament mounted on the wall. An intricate design reminiscent of the Star of David, yet distinctively unique in its craftsmanship, drew me in with its mystique and the whispers of stories it seemed to hold. The air was alive with the quiet murmurs of gentlemen clad in elegantly ironed black suits, their faces illuminated by the pale glow of their computer screens, absorbed in their tasks.

Suddenly, a random middle-aged man approached me, his presence almost magnetic. His graying hair framed a genial face adorned with a wide, inviting smile that suggested familiarity, as if he were an old friend. The warmth of his expression instantly put me at ease, making me wonder if perhaps we had crossed paths before or if he simply possessed an uncanny ability to make strangers feel welcome in this elegant, understated space.

"You must be Charles, am I right?"

"Yes, that is indeed me."

The Canadian member, whom I did not yet know,

stared oddly into my eyes.

"You might not remember me, but I remember you."

I tried to reset the clock and figure out who the man was, but it was impossible for me to remember him at that particular moment.

"Come, we have unfinished business to settle."

He led me to the elegant elevator and pressed the twelfth-floor button three times. The closing of the doors made a strange sound, almost as if it were locking us in. I am not at all claustrophobic, but the thought of getting stuck inside did cross my mind. We stood just a few feet away from each other, even though the elevator was wide. I could not help but ask about the status of Liam.

"Any concerns you have about any of the members shall be discussed on the twelfth floor."

I nodded in agreement due to the immense amount of respect that I had for him.

The elevator made an abrupt stop and the same strange noise I heard when the doors were closing. The man entered a couple of numbers rapidly. He turned to me, knowing that I was most likely shocked by what he had done. He recognized the expression on my face.

"Don't worry, just following the usual procedure."

I disguised my state of confusion with a slight smile. The numbers on the small display on the top turned green. The doors slid open; the member motioned with his hand to go in front of him.

I kindly accepted and proceeded to go first. The room was long and wide, filled with a display box of random historical objects and famous paintings mounted on the wall. I paused to better take in all the wonderful stuff in the room. My attention was caught by one of Abraham Lincoln's final speeches. The Canadian member walked behind me.

"Interesting, isn't it?"

He continued walking before I could give him an answer. My curiosity was so big that I didn't even mind my true objective. There were different sections in the room. I was in the ancient Rome section, which was indeed my favorite section. My brain could not process that the armor that was safely kept was real and not, in fact, a replica.

The Canadian member was at the far end of the room when the floor slowly started to rotate. I stopped everything to look around the room. I did not hesitate to turn towards the direction that the Canadian member was in.

"Don't worry, this is a disguise room; we meet behind these walls," he said while walking in my direction.

As he finished his sentence, the room stopped rotating, and we found ourselves suddenly somewhere entirely different. We were in a narrow hall with several doors on each side. I let the Canadian member step forward. He then turned around and told me to not move from where I was at. He proceeded to enter the second-to-last door that was on the left. A significant amount of time had passed, and the member had not yet come out of the room. Just when I was about to take a seat on the floor, he came out of the room while gesturing with his hand to come over.

It was finally time to step inside, and a rush of anticipation coursed through me, mingled with a twinge of nervousness, as I grappled with the unknown that lay ahead. The room before me was unassuming—its walls adorned with neutral colors and modest decor—but the true significance of the moment lay in the gathering of esteemed society members within its confines. As I crossed the threshold, my eyes were drawn to the figure of the Canadian leader, who held a commanding presence at the head of the long, polished table, radiating both authority and warmth. With a gracious attitude that reflected his status, he rose from his chair and extended his hand toward me, inviting me to take a seat. The gesture was one of generosity, and I felt a swell of pride at the honor of sitting alongside such distinguished, senior members of the society, whose achievements and wisdom echoed throughout the room. Their conversations buzzed with intellectual fervor, and I couldn't help but feel a sense of reverence wash over me, transforming the ordinary setting into a momentous occasion that I would carry with me forever.

"Charles, glad you could make it," the Canadian leader said, while I took a seat in the only empty spot. "As you know, there have been multiple attacks on our people. Multiple members of our society have disappeared all of a sudden."

Apart from his voice, the only thing to be heard was the slight noise of the air conditioner.

"The NEU wants us to release very dangerous men, powerful people, just like us," the leader kept explaining.

"What are we going to do then?" a member wearing a brown suit asked.

"Our failure to prevent the expansion of their union has put us in the position they wanted us to be." The Canadian leader said, Try to tell our men that we are in a very uncomfortable situation.

"I believe we shouldn't do it. We are giving them the tools they need to succeed," a member known by his last name, Johnson, said.

"Many of our men have been captured by them; some have even been killed. If they keep doing this to us, then they will eventually take over our society," the leader said.

"I have already spoken with the leader of the NEU. He agrees to stop their attacks on us if we give him what he wants."

"What will the future hold, then?" the man in the brown suit asked.

"No idea. For now, I believe we must yield and then regroup to see what action we are going to take," the leader announced, with a slightly concerned look.

CHAPTER 8

THE EXCHANGE

It turns out that the whole protest was just a way the Austrians had used to kidnap Liam. My lack of experience was on full display that very moment. Mistakes have always been important for my growth, but this one could cost my friend's life.

Liam did not hesitate to step out of his car to investigate the situation. He had only walked a few steps when the Austrians put a cotton pad over his nose, rendering him unconscious. From there, they took him to the nearest private airport that would fly him directly to Switzerland.

Unfamiliar with the specific composition of the pad's chemicals, I could nonetheless infer from the circumstances that the effects were quite intense. Liam did not awaken until the following morning, finding himself on the couch of a spacious yet elegantly adorned office. Despite the unusual nature of his situation, the environment exuded a sense of tranquility, likely enhanced by the incense sticks delicately arrayed around the room. Confusion was evident as Liam regained consciousness; he looked around, attempting to discern his surroundings.

At that moment, an elderly butler entered, presenting Liam with a tray of food. It was easy to imagine the extent of Liam's bewilderment. Lifting the lid from the tray revealed a rather elaborate meal. Despite his uncertainty about his whereabouts, hunger prevailed, and Liam began to eat without contemplating the potential implications of his actions. A few minutes later, the butler returned, having observed Liam's progress with the meal.

A figure entered the room shortly thereafter, casting a more imposing presence. It was none other than the leader of Austria, accompanied by several associates. Liam remained composed, directing his gaze towards the leader as he attempted to ascertain his identity. Two of the associates positioned themselves on either side of the leader, not as participants in the negotiation, but rather to act as a safeguard against any potential violent reactions from Liam.

"My apologies for the way I had to bring you in."

"Who are you?" Liam asked clearly, not knowing who the man was.

"I am the leader of the Austrian Society."

"If you're wondering why you're here, it's because Birkir kindly requested that I do this."

"Him again." Liam replied.

"You should thank him; if it weren't for him, I doubt you'd be alive."

"Why does he want me here?" Liam asked.

"We came to an agreement: we ensure your safety while you work with us."

"Why would I want to do that?" Liam asked, since he was not sure about the true intentions of the Austrian leader.

"To save your country from a possible collapse." The Austrian leader did not hesitate to reply.

"What makes you think that would happen?" Liam asked, while the leader of the Austrian society gave him a slight smirk.

"A terrifying partnership between your country and the NEU."

"No. We would never be interested in a partnership with them."

"That is what they want you to believe," the leader replied.

"Your country has always been seen as neutral and peaceful; for your leader and some of its members, this is seen as a sign of weakness."

"We have never been weak; when difficult decisions have arisen, we have always made the right choice. "

"That is what has been done traditionally, but with this new partnership, the way in which the society has been ruled will change." Liam found everything very difficult to soak. The leader of Austria would hand Liam an old flip phone.

"Once you have finished, call Birkir; he will explain everything in greater detail." The leader of the Austrian society said, before finally exiting the office with his members.

***

I could not have been any happier to find myself staying in a luxurious penthouse soaring high above the bustling heart of New York City. The night views were nothing short of breathtaking, with the city's skyline emerging in a dazzling cascade of twinkling lights that danced on the horizon like a sea of stars. The penthouse was a sanctuary of elegance, boasting an array of exquisite amenities that beckoned to be explored—each corner offering comfort and indulgence that made my short stay feel like a lavish escape.

Though I wasn't much of a drinker, the sight of the stunning bar caught my eye, its glossy surface reflecting the ambient light in a rich, warm glow. It was elegantly appointed with a selection of bottles that seemed to shimmer with promise, a testament to quality and craftsmanship. The bar's rich wood and polished brass accents added an air of sophistication, and I felt drawn to it like a moth to a flame. With a mix of curiosity and a touch of courage, I approached the bar and decided to treat myself by sampling a glass of Macallan whiskey, eager to discover if the velvety taste lived up to its luxurious price tag.

The temperature in the penthouse was just as I liked it—pleasantly cool, wrapping around me like a gentle embrace. I sank into the expansive, plush couch in the living room, its fabric soft and inviting, designed for comfort and relaxation. Before me loomed a massive flat-screen television, its sleek frame blending seamlessly into the modern aesthetic of the room. The space was beautifully appointed, with floor-to-ceiling windows that allowed the outside world to spill in, showcasing the vibrant energy of the city below.

All I wanted was to immerse myself in the luxuries of this sophisticated penthouse, relishing the solitude and tranquility it offered. The whiskey had surpassed my expectations, its rich, smooth flavor lingering on my palate and igniting a craving for another glass. With a sense of purpose, I rose and traversed the porcelain floor to return to the exquisite bar. Behind it, rows of premium spirits gleamed like jewels, and I poured myself another measure of the Macallan, savoring the way it glimmered amber in the low light.

After a moment of indulgence, an irresistible curiosity tugged at me—what might the view from the balcony reveal? I stepped outside, the fresh air wrapping around me like a cool balm. As I leaned over the railing, I was greeted by stunning vistas that stretched across the New York skyline, a breathtaking tapestry of twinkling lights and towering structures. The sights were almost surreal, captivating me with their splendor.

Slowly, I closed my eyes until an annoying light woke me up. I was not fully awake. Therefore, I did not know what was going on. Someone was holding me at gunpoint using a red dot sight. I remained in my chair, not knowing what to do. From behind me, I could hear footsteps slowly approaching me.

A tall, handsome man with brown hair stood before me. My head was spinning in endless circles, confused about who this man was.

"Mind if I take a seat?" the mysterious man with a Slavic accent said.

"It looks like I don't have much of a choice," I replied, according to his robotic personality.

He took a seat, along with a small sip of whiskey I had left over.

"Please, don't mind my friend here; he will only shoot if I tell him to."

Although it was a tense moment, the man was quite polite to me.

"If you want me to talk about my personal life, then you might as well tell your man to pull the trigger," I replied confidently.

"Now, why would I ask what I already know?"

Bits of information like this revealed to me that he was a society member; the question was, where was he from?

"How do you know me?" I asked, intending to uncover who he was.

"I am not here to discuss my life, Charles. I am here to save yours."

I looked at the red dot on my chest. The man gestured with his hand, and suddenly the red dot went away.

"Your society leader is deceiving you. He, along with his men, intends to join the NEU. They want you to believe they are being forced into it when they really aren't."

"What makes you certain?"

The Society member looked at me firmly in the eyes.

"In the past few months, twelve members of your society have been said to have been killed or kidnapped by the NEU. Have you wondered why?"

I shook my head in disagreement.

"The members who have been kidnapped had expressed their disagreement with the idea of joining the NEU," the unknown man said.

"What about the trade they are going to make?"

"The trade is a simple disguise to release all the corrupt people with radical beliefs."

"We believe they are going to kill you. I have placed a box on the bar with replicas of the guns that they'll use.

Your job is to switch them with the real ones before they find out."

"Why would they kill me?" I asked, confused as to what this man was telling me.

"Because you failed to betray your trainer. Therefore, they do not trust you."

At that moment, all I could think of was where in the world the red dot was coming from. I waited for a bit, giving the classified society members enough time to leave the building. After half an hour, I got up and headed straight to the bar, where the unknown man said he had placed the weapons. It took me a while, but I found a large black box well hidden behind the cabinets. Like always, I could not wait to reveal what it was. The guns were exactly like the ones we used. I quickly walked towards my backpack to compare the guns. Holding the guns side by side was the final exam. I needed to make sure that they were perfectly imitated.

***

Liam was situated in an enviable locale, nestled amidst the breathtaking panorama of the Swiss Alps, where the jagged peaks rose dramatically against the sky, cloaked in a velvet blanket of snow that glimmered in the golden light of dusk. The sunsets here painted the horizon in hues of crimson and violet, captivating in a way that rivaled the sweeping skyline I had admired from my luxurious penthouse in New York. To this day, I find myself puzzled over the Austrian Society's unwavering trust in him; what secrets lay beneath his calm exterior?

His accommodations were nothing short of lavish, a well-appointed guest room complete with an en suite bathroom that boasted marble tiles and a rain shower. A large flat-screen TV adorned the wall, streaming the latest updates from around the world, illuminating his face in flickering blue light during quiet evenings. Culinary delights were prepared just for him, crafted by the resident chef known for his culinary wizardry, whose expertise in international cuisine turned every meal into an exquisite feast that tantalized the palate.

Liam had the rare privilege of accessing the sprawling outdoor pool, its tranquil waters shimmering like jewels under the sun's rays. Yet, oddly enough, he had only taken a dip once during his brief stay. It was difficult to ignore the fact that he was only there for a matter of days, yet it was comforting to know he was in decent spirits, navigating this world of luxury and privilege.

As the shadows lengthened and the day began to surrender to twilight, the Austrian leader approached Liam three days later, the air thick with anticipation, just as the last rays of light cast an ethereal glow over the majestic landscape.

"Looks like you are not doing too bad," the Austrian leader said with a good heart.

"It could be worse," Liam replied.

"I would like to politely ask you for help," his words were genuinely said. The Austrian leader was by no means trying to lead Liam into doing something he didn't want. Liam noticed it and showed a willingness to collaborate.

"Please do," Liam said, trusting his intentions.

"There will be a political dinner tonight. Until now, everything appears to be fine. But you can never be too sure."

Liam turned his attention to the birds, who were chirping very loud.

"So… What do you want me to do?"

"Something I've heard you have a natural talent for."

"Surveillance," Liam answered, while the leader agreed with his head.

"You don't have to come if you do not want to." The Austrian leader gave him the choice, even though he needed Liam's assistance.

"Of course I will go. There is no reason for me to refuse."

This statement demonstrated that both men were comfortable being in one another's presence.

***

Given what had happened to me the previous night, it was hard for me to sleep. What the mysterious man told me was definitely something to keep anyone up at night. I required something to wake me up and get me ready for the day. I sat in the dining room, brainstorming possible ways to find out what society my unexpected visitor came from.

Since I needed to think deeper than I was, I took some time to relax and drink my cup of warm coffee in my room. Then, I went straight to my backpack, where I kept a fingerprint scanner that I had found back in the cabin. I was not hesitant to head to the table to test out the fingerprint scanner. I gently touched the top glass of the table to see how well it worked. The scanner could see what humans were unable to see with the naked eye. I pressed hard on the device, causing a sudden but luminous flash.

It was now time to search for the man's fingerprint. I went directly to the balcony area to scan the exact spot where he sat down. The fingerprint scanner worked marvelously, but I was unable to find anything. I tried again, but once more I got a negative result. Back inside, I found myself near the bar, where the man was most likely roaming around. It took me a while just to get nowhere; for twenty minutes I scanned the entire bar.

While at the bar, I poured myself a refined glass of whiskey. Although it was not the most appropriate moment for indulgence, I felt it necessary to help organize my thoughts. It took about three glasses of whiskey for me to piece together the puzzle. I retrieved the scanner and began to analyze the box where the firearms were stored. The device successfully captured a fingerprint, which I prompt-ly saved. Now, it was time to perform some technical oper-ations. I connected a USB cable from the scanning device to my computer. Two fingerprints appeared on the screen. I verified my own to confirm the system's functionality. Instantly, a report about me was generated, featuring pho-tographs from my childhood, before my training. I became somewhat distracted, inadvertently searching for infor-mation about my father rather than the member who had visited the previous day. As I mentioned earlier, it proved challenging to locate substantial information about my fa-ther. Nevertheless, I managed to uncover some missions he had undertaken, with one in particular catching my at-tention: it was called THE EXCHANGE. At times, my father traveled around the world to negotiate trade deals with other societies, exchanging valuable intelligence ser-vices for innovative tools that had yet to be developed by our own organization.

During that time, my biological mother was expect-ing a daughter but did not know the baby's gender before birth. Reports indicate that my father administered strong sedative medication to keep her calm, leading to a state of deep unconsciousness that left her unaware of her sur-roundings. Members of the society performed ultrasounds to ascertain the baby's gender and discovered they were ex-pecting a girl before she had any knowledge of this. Given the society's historical emphasis on maintaining a strictly male lineage, my father was compelled to undertake the difficult task of arranging an exchange. Since my mother was having a girl, he was instructed to find a male infant to replace her. This exchange was not a straightforward process. The Society mandated that the chosen child resemble the father genetically to prevent any suspicion from arising within the family unit. While engaged in this sensitive mission, my father received the necessary information and subsequently traveled to Moscow to retrieve a child from an adoption center. Unsurprisingly, he selected an infant that mirrored his own facial features.

After cautiously selecting me, he went to a clinic in Russia to see if I experienced any health problems that would stop me from becoming a member. The Society, with support from my father, helped deceive my mother into thinking that she was having a boy. My father returned to Canada, where I was under the custody of another unnamed member. Everything was precisely calculated up to the day that my mother gave birth, in the middle of the night. My father called the society members before sitting her on the dining room chair and giving her a glass of water. Subsequently, she would not recall the events that transpired, as she was sedated by my father. The members of the society came, fairly quickly, to my house. From there, they took her to an empty warehouse they had built as a hospital simulation room. My mother opened her eyes, and all she saw was me in her hands. As for the baby girl, she was handed to the Society, but there was no information about her. What I had just read was not at all easy for me to soak in.

***

Liam was preparing for his significant event. Although there were still a few hours until the actual dinner, he needed to get ready to impersonate a waiter. He donned a crisp, well-ironed white shirt, as his perfectionist nature compelled him to ensure that every detail was impeccable. He had an unusual habit of looking at himself in the mirror and placing a hand over his heart, a gesture he believed instilled him with the courage to face any challenge. After putting on his polished black shoes, he exited the room.

He walked all the way to the living room, where the Austrian leader was already waiting for him.

"Wow, you could not look any better," these were the first words the Austrian leader told Liam once he saw him.

"Save your flattery; I have looked better on different occasions," Liam replied in a light-hearted manner. The Austrian leader walked toward him to better adjust his bow tie.

"Your ride is outside; I need you to pay close attention to your surroundings," the Austrian leader said as he handed Liam a much newer phone.

"This is how I will be communicating with you. Make sure that you do not lose it."

Liam nodded, showing the Austrian leader that he had made himself clear.

Liam stepped outside and, eventually, into the vehicle.

***

I was at the penthouse, reviewing the details about the meeting between the Canadians and the NEU, when I received a message from the leader of Canada. They wanted to meet at a private house in about two hours. Finally, I had an excuse to leave the penthouse. I took the private elevator all the way to the first floor, where a friendly porter opened the door for me on the way out. The weather outside was a bit cold, but it was perfectly tolerable. I handed my keys to the young valet parking man. It was early noon, and there was no one requesting their car. He brought me to my car in a blur. The service was so good that I decided to tip him ten dollars. Luckily for me, I already knew my destination; the only thing that I hoped for was a smooth trip.

The house was quite a distance from the actual city. To my surprise, I arrived at the gated community without any issues. A tall, fit man came from the security hut to ask me for my identification. Like always, I complied with the rules. The man took my things and entered into the security hut. Nothing seemed wrong to me. Half an hour had passed, and there were still no signs of the man whom I trusted with my identification. I was getting a bit worried, so I decided to step out of my car to see what was going on. I walked towards the security hut, but the windows were tinted. Therefore, I could not see what was going on. I decided to knock on the door to let them know I was standing there. For safety measures, I took a few steps back. After ten more minutes, I had fully lost all my patience. I knocked on the door for a second time in a more forceful way. The security guy violently opened the door. I could not really see his face because he was wearing dark sunglasses.

"Why are you so rushed?" the security guard asked. Before I could even reply, he had tased me down to the ground.

I woke up in a state of great disorientation. I was well tied up to a chair. As I woke up, I saw the same young man who had come to my penthouse to warn me about both the NEU.

"Take this; it will, instantly, make you feel better," the man who had come to my house said, in a distinctive Slavic accent, while handing me a healing drink members of the Society usually drank. After almost drinking the entire glass, he did a discreet eyelid pull. This was a sign mostly used by European members to signal something is fake, although at that moment I did not know what it was.

Shortly after, a clean-shaven man in his sixties walked into the room.

"Charles, I've heard many things about you," the man said, while I would just stare into his eyes.

"Now tell me, Charles, who is it that you serve?"

"I believe you know the answer to that question," I replied.

"No. I don't, and besides, I want to hear it from you."

"I serve my country."

"What about your society? Do you serve them?"

"I don't feel the need to reply to that question."

The man took a brief pause to look at the rest of his members.

"Someone came by your house. Most likely to try to convince you that you should prevent any negotiations between the Canadian society and the NEU. Who is he? And don't lie to me; we know he placed a box containing replicas of your society's guns."

I could not be more confused, knowing that the man he was referencing was in the room.

"Even if I knew, I couldn't tell you for safety reasons."

The elderly man stared into my soul with his hazel eyes.

"We value your discretion, Charles. Although I must warn you, if you try anything to deter our deal, you and your whole family will suffer."

***

The fairy-tale-like village Liam was staying at was about two hours from Basel, where the fancy dinner was going to take place. Liam had a chauffeur drive him, which gave him peace. The tranquility inside the vehicle allowed him enough time to examine the dimensions of the building in a folder handed to him by one of his members on his way out. The well-dressed chauffeur kindly opened the rear door for Liam. The restaurant had incredible security measures, with high-end cameras everywhere you looked. Liam was checked with a handheld metal detector, but he already knew what to expect. At first, the interior did not seem like much, but once anyone started walking around the large halls, it was obvious that the event was for people of high status. Liam was professional and focused on his mission. Therefore, he did not get too distracted by the overwhelming luxury. He walked around the building to determine all the possible exits and entrances.

Simultaneously, he was placing the mini-microphones the Austrian Society had provided him with back at the house. The challenge was not performing the task. It was doing it discreetly, in a way that would not catch the attention of other employees working at the same time. Liam walked around the restaurant to see what exactly he was dealing with. He was asked by the event manager to help him properly set up the tables. This was not the most convenient thing, but it was something necessary for him to do. Liam spent almost two hours arranging the guest tables.

The work was semifinished, but Liam had not yet made sure that the place was safe. As he was walking out of the dining area, he ran into a security guard. Liam carefully looked around, just to see if anyone was following him. The guard led Liam into the monitoring room. He did not enter but watched the shift rotation. For Liam, this was his window of opportunity. Once more, he made sure that no one was watching him. He followed the security guard to his car, parked in an indoor garage. Liam was at a significant distance from the security guard. He proceeded to study the dimensions of the parking lot. An astute Liam found a way to run into the oblivious security guard. The guard was infuriated, but a sharp-minded Liam managed to cool the security officer. down. He needed to get the man's ID, the key into the monitoring room. He returned to the venue to face a big problem: he had to go through the security checkpoint once more.

There was a big line when he arrived, giving him just the right amount of time to put the identification card in his wallet. Liam managed to re-enter the venue without any trouble. There were a multitude of employees not wanting to be spotted by the manager. Liam headed directly to the kitchen, where he picked up a tray with three glass cups filled with water. He exited, intending not to be seen again. He walked directly towards the security room. I have no idea how, but he managed to pull out the ID from his pocket. He entered the small room to find one guard was sleeping and the other playing a game on his phone. Liam did not waste a second in pulling out his phone to connect with the devices in the room. He then picked up the tray of water and left as quickly as he could.

***

After the scary encounter with the leader with a Slavic accent, I found myself half-awake on the backside of a car. The rapid slaps of a thick hand woke me up abruptly. It was one of the Slavic men who escorted me out of the building that was driving me back to the penthouse.

"The boss wants me to tell you to remember to make the right decision." These were the final words I was told before I got out of the car.

I stood by the entrance of the penthouse, thinking that at least they had brought me back to my place. The porter was as kind as always. He opened the door with a smile from left to right. At the elevator, I started wondering, what is going on with my society? Numerous questions lingered in my brain, considering whether I was making the right decision or not. The doors opened into my luxury penthouse.

Once inside, I went into a vigorous search for the firearms the young man had left me. I failed to find them, most likely because they had been taken by the same people who had warned me not to interfere with their negotiations. I sat in a comfortable gray chair with a beautiful panoramic view of New York. For some reason, I could not help but think about the anonymous man who had warned me about my society. Not knowing who he actually was is what led me to find more information about him, using my iPad. I searched vigorously, but the only piece of information found was that his name was Malek; the remaining documents were blacked out, similar to the members of the society.

***

Even though Liam was under pressure, he was managing the situation like the genius that he was. He kept checking his personal phone, from which he had the entire building well monitored. It was just about three hours before the event. More and more people were passing by the checkpoint. It was too difficult to monitor everyone coming inside. However, Liam did his best to keep track of all the guests. Liam also took some time to check if there were any explosives hidden around the venue. He could not manage to scan all the walls, but everything seemed fine until this point. He continued his regular work.

Some guests were already in their seats. Liam did not mind making them feel like they were at home. The male guests were dressed in black tuxedos, and the female guests attended in expensive dresses. The room was only a quarter full of its capacity, but there were still many people in the dining area. Liam was working diligently, serving water to the tables where the high-status guests socialized among each other. Liam left the dining room when his jar of water was about to empty and bumped into his manager.

"Oh, Will, I need you to do me a favor and pick up an

order we made."

Society members rarely disclosed their true identities in public to ensure their safety. Liam was dissatisfied with being assigned an off-site duty; however, he recognized that compliance was necessary and had no choice but to accept the manager's directive. After returning the water jug to the kitchen, Liam proceeded to exit the premises. Outside, he found the manager awaiting him, accompanied by the employee responsible for driving him to the bakery.

Liam and the men barely spoke a word to each other on their way to the destination, and if they did, it was stuff that did not matter. On a positive note, Liam did get a chance to see the city of Basel a little more. To Liam's advantage and good fortune, they arrived earlier than he thought they would. The man parked just a few feet away from the bakery shop. Liam stepped out of the car, while his colleague remained seated. The car was stationed just across the street. Liam looked in both directions before crossing.

The bakery was open, yet empty. A complacent Liam entered the cute bakery. He walked towards the register, where there was no one yet in sight. Liam shouted hello, hoping for someone to respond. No one answered, even though he had called for someone multiple times. Liam was in a rush, but he decided to take his time, just in case someone eventually answered from the back room. He looked at his watch after ten minutes before deciding to look outside the shop, where the white vehicle remained in the same place.

Liam had waited enough and decided to enter the back storage room. There was nobody in sight. However, there was a horrid smell that almost caused Liam to leave the room. The room was dark and gloomy, and the kitchen lighting was not working properly. He used the flashlight on his phone for better visibility. The room was well organized, but it looked like somebody had just abandoned their work. Liam pointed the flashlight in multiple directions until he found the dead body of an elderly woman.

Liam became alert; the killer of the woman could still be somewhere in the room. He looked around like a wild hyena, but there was no one to be found. He exited the room to see if the vehicle was still there, which he was able to confirm simply by looking through the window. Something odd would take place, nonetheless, which is the fact that the vehicle blew up just a few minutes later. The explosion caused an injury to a mother walking along with her approximately seven-year-old daughter. Liam sprinted out of the room to assist them.

The young girl would not stop screaming. Liam tried his best to calm her down. However, she was too afraid to settle down. Multiple pedestrians nearby came to assist Liam.

It took a few minutes for multiple police cars to arrive at the scene. The paramedics checked Liam's state, but he was fine. The police approached Liam to ask him what had occurred. He explained everything from the beginning. The police were a bit concerned about the dead woman at the bakery. Liam showed a fake police identification on his personal phone for the officers to let him go. After showing his badge, the officers did not ask him any more questions. However, Liam had a major issue: how in the world was he going to get back without a vehicle of his own?

He could have easily arranged a ride, but at this point, he didn't have many choices. He walked away from the scene, just enough so that no one would recognize him. It took a while, but he managed to find an old sedan stationed away from the sight of everybody else. Liam carefully picked and locked the car with a toothpick he had obtained back at the event. Once inside the car, he hotwires the car, eventually turning the engine on, and leaves the scene.

CHAPTER 9

THE MEETING

The road back to the venue was, luckily, a safe one for Liam. He parked the car next to two luxury sedans. Even though Liam was a quick and analytical thinker, he was caught off guard this time. He did not understand what had just occurred to him. Liam took his time. However, he was not successful in trying to figure out what had actually happened. People were passing by as Liam stepped out of his car. He walked among the multitude of people. The moment was swift but harmful to an oblivious Liam. He could feel it, yet he was too slow to spot the man who had sliced him on his calf. He was not in pain, but blood came weeping rapidly from his leg. Liam understood that he could not enter the building with an injury, even with a minor one like the one he had. Intelligent, Liam knew that he was in an uncomfortable spot.

As Liam wove through the thrumming crowd, a surge of energy pulsed around him, a kaleidoscope of colors and voices blending into an indistinct backdrop. He took a moment to observe the scene, his keen eyes scanning the faces and movements of the throng, searching for any hint of danger. Utilizing his deft instincts, he deftly slipped away from the mass, ducking through a small, inconspicuous door that led to an unlit exit stairwell. Once inside, he secured the door behind him with a soft click, ensuring that no one could follow him through the entrance below.

Liam shifted his weight, pulling up his right legging to assess the wound that marred his skin. The cut was long and jagged, its edges still raw, but it wasn't the depth of the injury that unsettled him; rather, it was the unusual smell that wafted from it—an acrid scent that hinted at something far more sinister. A cold shiver ran down his spine as he contemplated the possibility of poison laced within the blade. If that was the case, his reflexes could fail at any moment, and the chilling thought coursed through him: he might not have long to act.

Time was slipping away like sand through his fingers. Recalling the stratagems honed in training, he swiftly unbuttoned his crisp white shirt, peeling it back to reveal a layer of simple cotton underneath. With urgency, he pressed his palm against the wound, applying pressure to stem the relentless flow of blood. Though the injury remained far from healed, he felt a sense of relief as the bleeding ceased, at least temporarily. Now, as the oppressive weight of uncertainty bore down on him, Liam steeled himself for the next phase of his mission, knowing that every second counted in his race against time.

This time, Liam took a different approach. He did not want to go through the checkpoint, so he carefully walked up the stairs. Liam safely managed to exit the room through one of the doors.

The place where the door led him was an unexpected one. Liam found himself in an abandoned conference room. The room was not in bad shape at all, but it had a strange aura. Liam took slow footsteps while trying his best to figure out the reason for that strange feeling. From a distance, Liam heard a slow clap and turned towards the direction where the noise was coming from. A man was standing just a few feet away from Liam. He was well groomed, using a cologne with a strong and pleasant smell that invaded the entire environment. This man owned multiple banks the Society worked with. He was known as Artek, but no one would dare mention his name, not even the most powerful society leaders. Liam was injured and did not have a weapon.

"I was hoping you'd be a little more menacing in person; you see, people like you are the reason the world is in a bad state," said Artek, and continued as he walked closer to Liam.

"I would give you a chance, but that would be a death wish for me." Liam remained in the same spot while Artek walked around in wide circles.

"Enjoy the rest of your night." Artek spoke with a tone that resembled that of declaring victory.

These were Artek's final words before exiting the building through the same place where Liam came in.

Liam looked around, knowing that he had been trapped. At this point, all the cards were against him, and he had nowhere to go. Even if he could not see it, he could hear the hazardous gas coming down from the air vent. A courageous Liam tried to find an exit. His pain worsened by the minute. The gas kept coming down at full speed; if he did not exit the room, then he would meet his demise. Liam walked to the other door, where he believed Artek entered through. He looked around the room, intending to find a pointy object to unlock the door. He tried his hardest, but his mind and body were not in the clearest of states. Liam's body was about to break down. He walked towards the door in an unbalanced manner and tried kicking the knob repeatedly, only to fall to the floor in pain. A random person suddenly opened the door while Liam was on the floor, fighting for his life. The person with a gas mask opened the door to drag him out of the room.

It took him a full day to recover from the toxic gas, which is why he had lost track of time. Once again, he woke up in a place he didn't recognize. Liam was in a small and unimpressive room with an insignificant window with blue and white curtains, small rays of sunlight passing through, revealing the dawn in all its intensity. He uncovered the sheet to look at his wound, which had been stitched. On the wall there was an old clock with Roman numerals; the time indicated was seven thirty-two AM, Liam imagined it from the sun. Liam left the room and walked straight to the living room, where he ran into a beautiful young woman keeping a glass tumbler on a well-crafted antique wooden shelf.

"Who are you?" Liam asked.

The startled woman slightly jumped, almost dropping the glass cup. He looked at her with a very slight grin on his face.

"What did you do to me?" he asked.

The lady finally put the glass cup on the top cabinet before replying.

"Three more minutes, and you would have been dead. You are lucky to be one of them. Otherwise, you would have been long gone," the woman kept performing the usual chores.

Liam curiously looked around the house.

"Is this your place?" Liam asked an odd question.

"I can only answer questions about your health."

The woman had finished all her chores.

"Take one of these every eight hours; it will help your

body remove the toxins," said the woman while handing him a pill container.

"Was my leg infected?" Liam asked while the woman looked at him fairly confused.

"Yes, you could have lost your leg."

Soon after that, the lady left the room. She shut the door closed, leaving Liam alone in the apartment.

***

I was in an entirely different situation. Things were not going perfectly for me, but I would not trade shoes with Liam. I suddenly did not know which side I was with. The following day, I arose without the desire to consume coffee and instead drank a bottle of sparkling water. There were many things I didn't know, or even understand, from the Society. It could be that I was still learning and needed to gain more knowledge to understand how things really work. After finishing my glass of water, I decided to sit on the living room couch. As I was heading to the balcony, my phone rang. The caller ID was private, which forced me to answer the phone immediately. The voice cut off a bit, so I had to pay close attention.

"We need you at the art gallery in 20 minutes. It is an emergency."

These were the words of the distorted voice. The conversation ended before I could even think of replying. I could not afford to waste time, so I went to my closet and changed into my casual clothes.

The valet parking staff was kind, like always. They took care of my car well, which I really appreciated. I got in my luxury car and drove directly to the art gallery. It was a miracle, too good to be true. When I arrived outside the art gallery, it was as clear as the sea; there was nobody in sight. The parking lot was also empty, which was also a green light. If you were to ask me, this was the first time that I had arrived early at any location. I went and bought an entrance ticket.

Each time I stepped into an art gallery, I was enveloped by the breathtaking array of masterpieces that hung upon the walls, each one a testament to the remarkable talents of artists from different generations and backgrounds. The air was thick with creativity, evoking a whirlwind of thoughts and feelings, as the vibrant colors and intricate details spoke to the depths of human experience. Art, I realized, is a profound means of expression; it weaves together varied emotions, inviting viewers to connect and share the tapestry of their life stories. This revelation struck me with greater clarity one afternoon when Jelena articulated it with such passion. I was incredibly happy to have arrived at the art gallery a few minutes before the big meeting.

I wandered through the gallery, my footsteps echoing softly on the polished floors, captivated and entranced, almost losing sight of my original purpose. In this particular space, a singular emotion permeated every canvas: freedom. It was palpable, as if the very essence of liberation danced through each brushstroke. Each artwork drew me in, commanding my attention and igniting my imagination, while the world beyond the gallery walls faded into a distant hum.

The museum was devoid of visitors, which worked to my advantage, allowing me to spot a member of the Canadian Society more easily. This absence of activity sparked a fleeting doubt in my mind: could it be a trap? I recalled that Society members could be recognized by their distinctive gait; they walked in a precise straight line for seven steps before deviating from that path—a practiced maneuver used to signal our presence to fellow members. As I continued my search through the vast, echoing halls of the building, I remained vigilant for any signs of the Society. After approximately ten minutes of searching, I finally spotted the individual I sought. To my surprise, it was a member of the Canadian Society whom I recognized from my childhood. It struck me as peculiar, for despite the years that had passed, the man appeared unchanged, as if time had stood still for him.

The man looked at me from top to bottom. Many people in the Society did this type of thing, but I did not know why. The man led me to the top floor, where we both stood in front of a beautiful painting. It was strange because we stood next to each other without saying a word for at least two minutes before the painting parted in different directions. Still in silence, the man gestured to me with his hand to go first. I did as I was told because I respected someone who had served society for many years.

The room was already filled, which was strange to me, given that I had arrived at the venue fairly early. Ten men were sitting at a beautiful round brown table. The Canadian leader kindly ordered me to take a seat. I took one of the two available seats.

"Gentlemen, thanks for coming, and pardon me for the unexpected meeting request, but something terrible has occurred."

Everyone in the room was laser-focused, paying attention to the Canadian leader.

"The leader of the Austrian Society has been killed."

The news was a big shock to me; things were only going to get harder.

"How does that affect us?" one of the members in the room asked.

"Although we have lost a great leader, we have gained peace of mind," the leader of Canada said.

"How so?" asked a random member in the room.

"We have one less leader judging our future decisions."

The room stayed silent, not sure about what the Canadian leader had just said.

"With all due respect, the death of a leader is something we shouldn't take advantage of; it is a worrying incident that makes us look fragile in front of other organizations." The member who looked at me on the way in made this statement, which I considered to be true.

"Not if we find out who is responsible for it and set an example to those organizations that believe they have gained an advantage over us." The leader said, letting everyone know that he is confident about his words.

"Who will take over the Austrian society, Know?" Another member asked, knowing that a potential change of leaders can be a dangerous thing.

"There are a few candidates I believe are fit to lead the country of Austria, but their society has not decided who will lead."

"Are there any more questions?" The leader asked, although the room remained silent.

"Good."

"One more thing before you leave. I wanted to remind you that our exchange will be happening in five days."

The meeting was over in just a few minutes from the previous statement. All the members were leaving the room, as was I. This was until the Canadian leader asked me to stay behind. The only emotion that I could feel at that moment was fear; I was afraid the Canadian leader knew something about me.

"Is there something wrong?"

I kept my composure simply because it was what I had been taught. However, I was not calm at all.

"Everything is fine, but thanks for your concern." I

replied, not wanting to draw any suspicions.

"My intuition tells me otherwise."

"I am just a bit tired, that's all." I replied while the leader nodded his head.

"Then tell me, what happened yesterday?" The Canadian leader did not hesitate to ask.

I did not have a choice but to tell the leader the truth of what had occurred.

"A leader from another society tricked me by sending a message as if it were you."

The Canadian leader's mood changed, all of a sudden, to a not very pleasant one.

"What did he look like?" the Canadian leader asked.

He looked at me for a slight second before adding, "A white man, with graying hair."

I simply replied with a slow nod.

"Were you planning to betray me?" the leader asked

"No, sir, I was planning on strategically protecting you."

The leader and I both exchanged intense eye contact.

"Good, you may leave," the leader said calmly.

I left the room not knowing what to expect from the Society. By that time, all the members had left the gallery, giving me somewhat of an escape from the terrifying confession I made to one of the most powerful leaders in the world. I don't know why, but I had a feeling that I was going to be punished, even though I had not revealed much information about the Canadian Society.

A group of young students was entering the building as I was exiting it. I turned around because it reminded me of when I was a kid. At that moment, I remembered that Liam was not in the best of positions; I didn't even know if he was alive, for that matter. The combination of anxiety and concern caused me to forget where I had parked my car. I was able to find my car after a few minutes. I started the car; the engine made a strange noise, one that it had not previously made.

Traffic on the way back was not too bad. It was almost noon, and as I had not had breakfast, I decided to stop for some brunch. New York had various restaurants to choose from, but I was feeling like a good American brunch. Even though it was a day full of challenges, something odd made me smile. It was the fact that I was able to find a spot to park my car at the mall, which was busy at any time of the day.

There was something remarkable about American malls. Every time anyone passed by a small kiosk, the employees were eager to sell their product. After passing by the obnoxious salespeople, I walked to the back, to the restaurant area. There were many options to select from. However, I went with my initial choice, which was American cuisine. The interior design of the restaurants was like walking inside a time machine. It reminded me of the time my father took me for dinner just before I commenced my training. A kind African-American woman led me to a seat in the back. The restaurant was slightly busy, which made it fine for me to relax. An elderly man approached my table.

"What would you like to drink, sir?"

"I'll have a Coke with plenty of ice and a straw," I answered.

"Right away," the kind man replied.

I found myself with little to occupy my time, and truthfully, I was unwilling to invite any further complications beyond those I had encountered lately. For some reason, my thoughts remained preoccupied with the potential repercussions of my situation. Gradually, I began to appreciate the ambiance of the establishment, which was rather pleasant. The walls adorned with images of various rock and roll legends evoked fond memories of a similar place I had visited with my father many years ago. At that moment, the waiter returned to my table, carrying a single glass delicately balanced on a tray, which he placed with care before me.

"Do you know what you would like to order?"

I was so caught up on other things that I had completely forgotten to take a look at the menu.

"Sorry, I was daydreaming," I told the man in complete shame.

"No problem, just let me know when you are ready," said the man before leaving.

There were numerous options available to choose

from. Since my earliest memories, I have had a deep appreciation for American cuisine, and I have always been particularly impressed by the diverse range of dishes. After careful consideration, I finally reached my decision. It is advisable to remain aware of one's surroundings at all times. Consequently, I paid a significant price when I finally set the menu down, only to find Malek—the same young man who had previously cautioned me about the intentions of my society—sitting directly across from me.

"Wow! I see that a friend has joined you. Would you like something to drink, sir?" the polite waiter asked.

"A strawberry iced tea, please," Malek replied.

"Sure, right away!" the waiter said before he left.

Even though Malek was working with a dangerous group of people, I did not feel threatened by his random appearance.

"So, why the unexpected visit?" I asked before taking a sip.

"I like to warn my friends," Malek said, while I made a strange facial expression.

"Who do you work for?" I asked.

"Now, I'm sure you know public places like this are not ideal to ask questions like that," Malek intelligently replied.

"While you were at the meeting, members of your society planted an explosive in your car."

Before making this statement in a very low tone of

voice, Malek looked around.

"Are you guys ready to order?" the elderly waiter asked, luckily just a few minutes after Malek had finally finished his statement.

"Yes, I will have a Caesar salad with grilled chicken," Malek replied.

"Perfect, and you, sir?"

"I will have a medium-rare sirloin with mixed vegetables."

"Alright. I will get that ordered," the waiter said before leaving.

The situations were difficult for both of us. However, that was not going to stop us from spending some time together. Even though the restaurant was not too busy, it took a while for the food to be delivered to us. The kind waiter brought us a complimentary basket of bread due to the unexpected waiting time. While we enjoyed the variety of breads, Malek and I had a good time chatting with one another. We were professionals; therefore, we did not reveal any classified information about our respective societies. I was curious to know Malek's journey to becoming a member. The training from his society was not very different from mine. The only thing that would separate us was the fact that they had to learn more languages than we did. It made sense to me, given that they were in Europe, and they had to communicate with foreigners who spoke different languages.

Upon my arrival at the restaurant, I had anticipated a distinct experience; however, I must admit that I thoroughly enjoyed Malek's company. After half an hour, the waiter came with our food. My sirloin steak was medium-rare, just as I liked it, while Malek's salad was plain, but he did seem to enjoy it. The kind waiter came to pick up our plates and asked us if we wanted any dessert. Both of us refused, having no room for dessert. The man came right away with the bill. I was going to pay it, but Malek stopped me. So he could pay in cash.

After the payment was complete, Malek explained to me that it was crucial to always pay in cash if you wanted to be incognito. We stayed a little longer to discuss how we were going to handle our tricky situation.

"The bomb will go off a few minutes after you set foot in your car."

It was strange because I was composed yet concerned at the same time.

"Did you try deprogramming it?" I asked, thinking that maybe there was a slight chance.

"If we do, then they will know you are still alive."

I did not reply, but I did think that he had a point.

"What shall I do then?" I asked, putting my full trust in Malek.

"Stay calm, and follow my orders." Malek spoke, convinced that his plan would succeed.

"Can anyone be harmed due to the explosion?"

Charles asked, referring to the Canadian citizens who are around once the bomb goes off.

"We are uncertain; however, in circumstances such as these, our options are limited," Malek replied, while Charles was doing his best to hide his deep concern.

"The radio of the vehicle will activate a red light that will buy us some time. Once you see a white van, open the passenger door and get inside. Understood?" Malek asked to check if I had indeed grasped the entire mission.

The difficulty of the mission left me speechless. Nevertheless, I nodded, letting Malek know that I had understood everything he had told me.

Malek left before I did, although I do not know what exit he took. Just from spending a little time with him, I knew that he had experience dealing with these sorts of things. If I had learned one thing from Society, it was that you can never be too sure about the things that surround you. I looked around the restaurant to check if there was anything suspicious. The place was a bit busier than when I entered; however, there were no signs of trouble. I carefully left the place a few minutes after Malek left.

It was a delight to walk back to my car without any issues. I took a deep breath before starting the engine for one last time. Things were difficult to understand; however, I had to see the bigger picture. I had a big test ahead of me, and therefore I had to get myself ready to tackle a huge task. The car did not make the strange sound that it made the last time. I looked at the time on the radio, just to make sure I was on the right track. The streets were jam-packed with traffic, and all I could think about were innocent lives that could be lost in the hands of my people.

I was among a multitude of cars, calm but worried that I would not make it on time. The traffic was moving, but at a very slow pace. I looked at the clock, and ten minutes had passed. The clock was ticking, and I was getting more anxious by the second. It wasn't what I was supposed to do, but it was one of the few options I had. When it was my turn to go through the traffic light, I took a right turn instead. The road was clearer on this end. I wanted to call Malek, but I didn't, knowing that the Society could be listening to our conversations. Even though the hourglass was shifting against me, I tried my best to continue with the intended plan. I had no choice but to drive as fast as I could to reach my destination.

Suddenly, I turned into a professional race driver. It was not something I would usually do, but I must admit it was quite fun. It was a great relief to know I had arrived at the stop where the van would be. Just a few seconds later, I turned on the radio, like Malek had instructed me. There was an issue; I had not spotted the white van yet. Everything was fine with the car nevertheless. Once I spotted the white van, it was like seeing an oasis in the middle of the desert.

By that time, I was already in the passenger seat, ready

to leave. The white van was stationed next to me. The streets were busy. I took a deep breath before slowly opening the passenger door. Even though I was outside the car, I was slow to get in the van. The passenger seats of the van were empty. The traffic light changed, and the van took off. I did not see it, but, from a distance, I heard the car exploding. At that moment, I could only think about Malek, who had gone out of his way to save my life. It was obvious that we were heading to a certain location, although I didn't know where exactly. I had the entire row of seats all to myself, making a long trip enjoyable. The van came to a full stop after around 40 minutes. The chauffeur, whom I didn't know, slid the door open, revealing a long driveway that led us to a beautiful two-story mansion. The lawn was well-maintained, and the front porch was impeccable.

I was being led by my apparent driver. The man stood by the door and looked closely through the peephole. It did not take long for someone to let us both through. I hesitantly walked inside the mansion, where many members of Malek's Society were waiting for both of us. All the men began to clap simultaneously. The few members that I saw gave me a blank look. I finally stood before Malek, who nodded, most likely happy I had trusted him.

Malek led me to a spacious office, where the leader of his society was sitting. My trust was not one hundred percent devoted to his leader. However, I had to thank them for saving my life.

"You are lucky to be alive," the leader of the Society said while sitting face-to-face with me.

"I am grateful that you have risked your members to save me."

Even though he did not say anything, it was obvious that the leader was complacent about what I had said.

"Would you like to work with us?" the leader asked.

"I would like to, but not before I know whom I am working for."

"All the men inside this house belong to the Polish Society. Now it is up to you to decide if you would like to work with us," the leader of the Polish Society said, very assertively.

CHAPTER 10

LIFE OF SUPRISES

When I became a member, I had no clue about what was going to happen. Trust was something I learned back when I was training to become eligible for the Society. It was important to be reliable. However, there would be many instances when members would have to put their trust in other people's hands. Once you become a member, you find it difficult to trust anyone. I was unsure why the Polish Society believed I would not turn on them. But I could not have been more grateful for their actions.

However, there was still something that bothered me. After what had occurred at my parents' house, I was not certain about the safety of my family. It was not until my third day that Malek joined me while I was sitting on the terrace.

"Is something concerning you?" Malek asked.

I replied by simply nodding.

"What troubles you?" Malek asked, not knowing what to expect.

"I fear they will go after my family," I told Malek. Worried.

"Do you trust me?" Malek asked me.

"I have faith in you, but I do not have faith in my people."

After the conversation ended, the leader of the Polish Society joined us.

"What is going on here?"

Neither of us displayed our emotions, but we were surely very nervous to be around the leader. I looked at Malek, trying to ask him not to reveal anything that we had discussed.

"Our friend is worried about the lives of his loved ones."

The Polish leader and Malek made eye contact.

"Has Malek not told you yet?"

I looked at the Polish leader, confused.

"Your family is under my protection. If something were to occur, we will hunt the person responsible for hurting the ones you love."

The words were powerful and provided me with the right peace of mind. The Polish leader hand-signaled to the butler, who walked directly toward us.

"A bottle of champagne, please."

The butler nodded before leaving the table.

***

Liam found himself in one of the apartment rooms, still grappling with the mystery of how he had arrived there. He had somewhat alleviated his pain, recognizing that rest was essential for a swift recovery. However, this proved challenging for someone who had always been inherently energetic. He occupied his time with a laptop he had discovered, although reports regarding the previous day's events remained elusive.

Everything seemed fine until a strange noise caught Liam's attention. It sounded like someone was trying to sneak inside the house. Liam did not waste time preparing himself for war. His instincts did not fail him; he had heard enough to know that someone did indeed enter the apartment. Liam knew that being injured was a disadvantage. He stood at a significant distance from the door so that the intruder would not know his position, which gave him a chance to defend himself. Liam held his breath as much as he could. He could hear gentle footsteps approaching his location. It was evident that whoever might have entered the house was cautious and did not want to be heard. The moment of truth arrived. Liam had no option but to fight for his life. The random person slowly opened the door and entered the room that Liam was in, although they hadn't seen him. The man was halfway inside the room. Liam did not waste time disarming him of his pistol. The man, most likely a member, kicked Liam in the hand he was holding his gun with, causing the gun to go flying in a different direction. Liam was in a difficult situation; now he had to fight the man one-on-one. The man aggressively hit Liam in different parts of his body. Despite Liam's proficiency in self-defense, he was still disadvantaged and required various maneuvers to maintain his balance. However, Liam was moving strategically. His opponent was so focused on trying to take him down that he hadn't considered where he had dropped his gun. Liam got both of them in the perfect position for him to grab the man's gun.

"Who sent you?" Liam asked while holding the man at gunpoint.

From the looks of it, the man did not care too much about Liam's question. He had one goal, and not even the fear of his demise would prevent him from doing anything else.

Even though it was hard for Liam, he didn't have a choice. He shot the man down until he was dead. We were well-trained, but killing was always the last resort. Liam sat on the floor. Yet again, someone else entered the apartment. For some reason, Liam did not seem as worried about this person coming in. The woman entered the room, shocked to see the disturbing sight of the man dead on the floor.

The woman helped a worn-out Liam to the living room couch, where he lay down. She returned to the room to grab a small first aid kit. She injected Liam with a special antibiotic to relieve the toxins from his body. The medicine was so strong that it made him go to sleep in a matter of seconds.

Liam was not his usual self; until that very moment he had never been as vulnerable. He managed to wake up after six hours, feeling better. It took him about a minute to notice the Austrian members standing around the living room. Liam was starting to recover, but he was not in the mood to deal with anyone.

"Close call," said Friedrich, whom Liam had previously met at the conference.

"You didn't happen to order my assassination, did you?" Liam said in a sarcastic manner.

"No, if I wanted to do that, I would have made a bigger spectacle." Friedrich replied, making a cheeky reference to what occurred at the conference of nations.

"I have found out I don't enjoy spectacles too much."

"Then we are on the same page," Friedrich replied.

"It was them, wasn't it?" Liam asked, believing that the men who tried to kill them were working with the NEU.

"That's what we think, but we are not one hundred percent sure."

"Are you in pain?" Friedrich asked.

"Physically just a little, but mentally I am concerned about what the future holds."

"Get some rest; we will discuss our plans with you some other time," Friedrich said, signaling the rest of the men to leave Liam alone.

***

I have been incredibly fortunate to experience stays in remarkable locations, including this stunning mansion and an opulent penthouse. During my brief tenure as a member, I have come to realize that the society as a whole is indeed exceptionally affluent. Being a deep sleeper, I naturally awoke early the following morning after the previous evening's marvelous events. Rising from my plush bed, I made my way to the mini-bar, where I selected a soft drink before settling into the inviting chair on the balcony. The ambiance within the house was wonderfully tranquil, while the attentive staff tended to the vibrant flowers in the garden below. Reflecting on my journey, I acknowledged the diligent efforts I had invested since childhood to reach this point; yet, I found myself questioning whether it had all been worthwhile. Joining the Society had proven to be a significant source of frustration, but I remained hopeful, clinging to the belief that this tumultuous chapter would eventually come to a positive resolution.

At times, it was difficult for me to control my emotions. I had been told by Malek and the leader that my family would be fine, but for some reason, I was not one hundred percent sure that what they were saying was true. I walked the halls of the house, thinking if I should leave and check on my parents. Something was stopping me, however; it was the distance separating me and my home back in Canada. I sat in the living room all by myself. It was not long before the leader sat by my side.

"You're up early," the Polish leader said.

"I slept well."

"Sleeping is good for you. It fuels the brain," the Polish leader explained, giving good words of advice.

"Good. I am still mentally weak."

"Don't worry. We were all there at some point," the Polish leader replied.

One of the many servants in the house came to ask us if we wanted something to drink. Coincidentally, we both asked for water; he graciously served it to us in a beautiful crystal glass that was on a table at the side of the room. Asking permission in a somewhat confused accent, he left in the direction of the kitchen. I was hesitant to share my thoughts, mainly because I lack extensive knowledge, but something seemed off. The servant was young, and despite his clothes, he was clearly physically prepared. From the way he spoke, I could tell he wasn't American. It is true that there were numerous immigrants in America; however, the individual in question gave me the impression that he was concealing something. My temptation was almost greater than mine, but I did not dare to make a mistake.

The mansion was so big that he still didn't know where all the rooms were.

In an effort to gather more information about this man, I approached the Polish leader and inquired about the location of the nearest restroom. He directed me to a facility adjacent to a recreational area. Upon entering the bathroom, I was uncertain of what to expect. It was purely coincidental that the restroom featured two distinct exits. I took a moment to wash my face and gaze into the mirror, attempting to buy myself some time. However, confronting my reflection was unnerving; for me, a mirror was a stark vessel of truth, revealing realities that often contradicted my desires. Despite my internal conflicts, I remained resolute in my primary objective. Consequently, I chose to exit through the alternate door, which led me to the exterior of the house.

Walking outside the house was always a pleasure. The beautiful, well-trimmed grass was a gift from nature to humans. There was a team of landscapers taking care of the vibrant garden. Even though it was a sight worth seeing, my focus was on my objective, which was trying to determine if my accusations were true.

I quickly managed to find the kitchen, where the small staff was working. The man was at a distance from where I was. I remained in a spot where I knew the man was unable to see me. Fortunately, I did not hinder the employees of the kitchen. Once the man exited the kitchen, I continued by following him at a distance. From the looks of it, the man looked harmless. I attempted to see whether the man had any weapons with him or not. However, if he was well-trained by one of the societies or any other organization for that matter, it would be difficult to determine whether he was armed.

After following the man for a short amount of time, he finally reached the living room where the Polish leader was.

"Stop!" I said, approaching the Polish leader, who was oblivious of my true intentions.

Everyone did as I said. Both the men were confused by my words.

"None of us will drink from the water until you do."

I was in no position to request this, but I had to make sure this man was not a spy.

"With all due respect, sir, it would be rude to do so," the servant replied in an educated fashion.

Although he did not display it, the Polish leader was becoming more skeptical by the second.

"You will do as I say," I told the servant, while the leader gave me a serious glance.

The servant had no choice but to do as he was told. He grabbed the bottle of water slowly and confidently. Everything seemed fine until he threw the water into the face of the Polish leader, burning his eyes. I left the leader's side to follow the servant, who sprinted out of the scene.

It didn't take me long to slip into his feet like a soccer player, lowering him to the ground. The individual who arose from the ground at a rapid pace was most likely a member of a distinct society. He tried to kick me in the head; luckily, I dodged his kick. The fight continued for a little longer, until he used a taser, which brought me down to the ground. The arrogant servant kept on tasing me while I was on the ground. This was until Malek came and shot the man multiple times. Seconds later, Malek helped me up off the ground, which was helpful since I was significantly dizzy.

"Do you know who he works for?" I asked, wondering if Malek knew anything.

"No idea, but this will help us," Malek replied while gathering a bit of his blood.

"Let's go, we need to remove your makeup," Malek told me, referring to the blood that was slowly pouring down my nose

We were fortunate to have a medic on site. The middle-aged man took care of both me and the Polish leader. Not knowing what the water the servant had thrown onto his face contained, the medic took care of the leader first before helping me out. The medic was only there for minor reasons, so he was not sure of what was actually in the liquid. The eyes of the leader were fine, although he did mention he had a slight headache. Malek and the rest of the members were extremely concerned about the health of their leader. They were so into what had happened to their leader that they did not look at me for a split second. This was something that I found inspiring because it indicated that this society was a real brotherhood. It took longer to cure the leader than to cure me. I did not want them to waste too much time on me, either, because I knew we had to get down to business. Before the medic left, he handed the leader a medication and advised him to take it if his headache did not go away.

Shortly after, all the members gathered in the large conference room where they would usually meet.

"Well, what a way to start the morning, gentlemen!" the Polish leader said with a bit of humor. "It looks like our enemies tried to get the better of us."

The leader was, indeed, proud to make the statement, knowing that they had failed in their attempt on his life. I, on the other hand, was worried, thinking that there could be other possible spies on site.

"Who was the man, sir?" Cisek, a loyal member of the Polish Society, kindly asked.

"Malek, can you answer that question?" the leader asked.

"Yes, sir. His name was Bogdan, and he was a member of the NEU," Malek replied while looking at his electronic tablet.

"So, the NEU has infiltrated our home," the leader of the Polish Society made the interesting remark.

"Yes, that is what the system is telling me, sir."

I do not know why, but the leader seemed skeptical. Everyone in the room noticed his awkward silence, along with his facial expressions. The leader seemed mad, although he was hiding it with a great poker face.

"Malek, how did they know about our location?" the leader asked while menacingly walking around the room.

"With all due respect, sir, I believe you know the answer," Malek replied, as respectfully as he could.

"Are you trying to tell me there is an informant in this room?"

Everyone in the room was silent, most likely frightened.

"I ask for the person responsible to rise from their seat," the leader of the Polish Society said, while standing in one place.

The tension in the room had reached its peak. The leader waited for a moment, but no one had the courage to get up.

"Malek, who do you think has betrayed us?" the Polish leader put Malek in the most uncomfortable position.

"I believe there is a traitor, but they are not in this room."

The Polish leader made direct eye contact with Malek, who did not want to expose any of his members.

"Who in here has Soviet blood?" the Polish leader said, referring to the countries that comprised the old Soviet Union.

"Sir, why don't we leave this for some other time?" Hans, one of his most loyal men, said.

"If we leave this for another time, then our enemies will have the edge," the reluctant leader answered.

One of the members stood up from his chair. Nobody saw it coming, leaving everyone in the room in complete disbelief. The leader was composed but disappointed at one of his youngest members.

"Why did you do it?" the leader asked.

"I didn't want to…"

"I did not ask you if you wanted to do it; I asked why," the leader asked angrily, clearly out of patience.

"They threatened my mother, sir," the young member said, ashamed of himself.

The leader of the Polish Society looked at Malek.

"Do what you have to do," the young man said, with no regrets.

The Polish leader took a deep breath before sitting back down on his chair. The young traitor remained on his feet while the room was silent.

"Tell me, gentlemen, what should we do with this disgusting human?"

Even though I thought that the leader of the Polish Society was a good man, I did not like his comment at all.

I looked at the men, who looked like mannequins.

"I am giving him a chance; if you stay quiet, then I will

decide his fate."

Nobody in the room replied. The leader looked around and nodded.

"Hand me your gun, Bacic."

I looked around, sort of astonished that none of the members had stood up for the young man. Bacic had no option but to hand the leader a shiny Beretta gun.

The young man closed his eyes while the leader of Poland was holding him at gunpoint.

"Wait!" Malek said before the leader of Poland could pull the trigger.

"This man deserves a second chance. It is true that he has betrayed our oath, but he should not pay with his life. His grandfather died to protect our society and make sure it remains in power. If there is anyone to blame, it should be us for not taking cautionary measures. "

Everyone in the room turned their attention towards Malek.

"So you believe this man should live?" The Polish leader asked.

"Yes, he was forced to choose between his mother and his country. Being a member of this society, I believe he was going to decide to protect both of us. " Malek firmly replied.

The Polish leader was not too complacent about Malek's statement. The room was silent, and the leader was still holding the man at gunpoint. However, it was a great delight to see the leader spare the life of the young man.

"Everyone, leave. Except for Charles and Malek," the leader said.

All the members left at once. Malek and I were the only ones who remained in the room. I was feeling bad because I was the one who suggested not to kill the man who had betrayed his people.

"Are there more of them?" the Polish leader asked me.

"I believe…"

"I was asking Charles," the Polish leader said.

"There may be."

The leader of Poland looked at Malek, then he turned his attention towards me.

"What do you suggest we do?"

"We need to calm down and act in a measured manner, not to raise suspicions."

"How many more do you think there are?" Malek asked.

"Just one, and it is most likely a woman."

The leader looked at me disgusted, not necessarily at me, but at the fact that the NEU had used women to spy on us.

"We are going to need a plan if we want to find out who the spies are," Malek said.

"No, we don't have time." I said, to express the level of urgency that we must have.

"Charles, it looks like you have a good eye. I will leave it to you to find the remaining spy."

"Yes, sir," I said firmly.

***

Liam was still resting in the apartment. He was almost fully recovered. However, he did not have much of a spirit to do anything but watch some TV. Liam was well-trained and always aware of any signs of danger, just like I was. Even though we got along, we each had a unique skill set. Nonetheless, a peculiar connection emerged between us immediately upon our encounter. It was not long before Friedrich, along with his members, entered the house.

"Something tells me you are feeling better," Friedrich said.

"Thanks to you, I am," Liam replied, happy to have received a helping hand.

"I want to give you an opportunity, Liam, one I think you will accept."

"Please don't hesitate to let me know," Liam did not hesitate to reply.

"My man and I have arranged a safe place, somewhere you will be forgotten by the society."

"You want me to renounce my oath to my country." Liam asked, surprised by what was being proposed to him.

"I want you to live a peaceful life," Friedrich replied.

"My life can't be peaceful if my country isn't safe.

Thank you, but I must kindly deny your offer." Liam told Friedrich, who was proud to hear that Liam was loyal to his country.

"Have you heard the news?" the Austrian member asked, thinking that Liam might already know what had occurred.

"I've heard many," Liam said,

Friedrich looked at the surrounding members, who really didn't mind Liam's sense of humor.

"Our leader has died," Friedrich said.

"Was he killed at the event?" Liam asked.

"Yes, and we believe it was by one of your men."

"My men? Are you saying we are working with the wrong people?" Liam articulated this thought, both confused and disturbed.

"We had suspected it, but now, I believe we have confirmed it," Friedrich said.

"Why didn't you tell me?" Liam asked.

"We were not sure. That's why I need you to come with me, to confirm what we have believed for a long time."

Liam did not say a word. However, his look said it all.

"If he is, in fact, one of our members, will you kill him?" Liam asked, most likely because it would have been extremely tough for him to see one of his members get killed in front of his eyes.

"No, he will be trialed for the death of an all-powerful leader."

"Take your time; we will wait for you outside," Friedrich remarked, noticing that Liam was in a very difficult situation.

Friedrich did not need to say anything to the members surrounding the house. Liam was left alone in sheer disbelief. When we make the vow in front of the Society, we swear to protect our people and our country at all costs. The vow made it incredibly difficult for Liam to acknowledge the truth. It was no easy decision for him; however, after some time of reflection, he decided to do what was right. Liam got up from the sofa and headed to the closet, where he had a pair of black pants and a blue shirt. It did not take long for Liam to get ready; he grabbed the P-96 pistol he had taken from the man who tried to take his life.

All the members were standing around, seemingly not doing much, but fully aware of everything happening around them. Liam walked to where Friedrich was, standing alone by his luxury SUV.

"Thank you, Liam," Friedrich said, who perhaps was one of the most loyal and kind men in the Austrian Society.

"I would like to drive to the destination myself. If you don't mind." Liam requested, just in case anything went south.

"How would you manage that?" Friedrich asked, knowing very well that Liam did not have accessible transportation.

"I have my ways; just tell me where you will be, and

you have my word that I will indeed be there."

Friedrich extended his hand, and Liam accepted it, adding more value to his words.

All the Austrian Society's vehicles had left. Before, Liam brainstormed ways in which he could find a car. He stood with his back against the wall of the building that he was staying in. During a short amount of time, Liam would simply clear his head from all the recent troubles. Fortunately for him, he managed to erase everything. Liam was a man who did not like to break promises. Therefore, he walked the beautiful little town, hoping he would find a way in which he could head to Friedrich's destination on his terms.

A few minutes in, Liam was incredibly fortunate to have found a man outside a car rental business. On the flip side of things, the man was apparently closing the store.

"Sorry, we are closed," the man said as Liam mildly sprinted towards him.

"Can you make an exception?" Liam kindly asked.

"Unfortunately, no, I have already checked out." The man left Liam in complete despair at that precise moment.

"I will offer you my watch if you let me rent a car," Liam offered while following the man, who had no intentions of helping.

The man stopped to look at the expensive Cartier watch, which was enough to convince him to head back to the store.

In a matter of seconds, the man opened the store and immediately turned on the lights. The place inside was a bit small, but Liam did not mind; all he wanted was to resolve his minor problem. Witnessing the man take his time to start the computer gave Liam a good understanding as to why the man was reluctant to rent him a car.

"What car would you like?" the rental man asked.

"Something fast."

The man could only smile at Liam's request.

The rental agent and Liam exited the store and made their way to the parking lot to explore the available options. While there were numerous vehicles to choose from, the selection of sports cars was somewhat limited. Liam quickly gravitated towards an orange Corvette, as orange was one of his favorite colors. They then proceeded back to the office to finalize the rental paperwork. Fortunately, the process was efficient and did not take long, after which the agent handed Liam the keys to the vehicle.

Liam and the rental agent bid each other farewell. Although Liam had experienced numerous high-end vehicles in the past, this occasion felt distinctly different. His enthusiasm for sports cars mirrored my own, yet he remained focused, aware of the challenging circumstances that lay ahead. When he ignited the engine, it roared to life, filling the air with a powerful sound. He then retrieved a crumpled piece of paper from his pocket, which contained the address he needed to navigate to.

The road leading to his destination was clear, but the sunlight was gradually waning. Liam activated the car heater, seeking relief from the slight chill in the air. He was not particularly fond of music and instead found himself deep in thought, aware that his loyalty was about to be put to the test. After approximately one hour and thirty minutes, Liam reached his destination: a sparsely populated village dotted with a few houses. Following Friedrich's strict instructions, he parked the car at a considerable distance from the main residence.

Exiting the comfortable vehicle, he was greeted by the now brisk weather. The winds were fierce, and the village resembled a ghost town in its eerie stillness. Undeterred, Liam continued along the rocky path toward the house, moving directly toward the trees. While the atmosphere might have unnerved others, Liam remained calm; he had undergone training in the forest, where darkness was commonplace. After walking roughly a mile, he was approached by two Austrian guards, who conducted a thorough check. Liam remained unfazed by this encounter, as he had nothing to conceal apart from the pistol he had brought along for protection.

"What is this?" one of the members asked when they found out Liam was carrying a weapon.

"It is hard for someone like me not to carry a weapon after they tried to take my life," Liam said in the politest but most honest way possible.

The men let him in without his gun. Liam was ready for anything, but people like us found it incredibly challenging to put our trust in others.

The house was almost like a French château. From what I've heard, it was bigger than the one I was staying at. The front porch of the house was lit by a yellow chandelier. It was only a matter of time before one of the members, who had gone to the house earlier on, led the way for Liam. The inside of the house was like going back in time; everything was old and rustic, yet elegant. Liam was taken to an old wine cellar, where all the members were standing around, including a man who had not yet been identified, wearing a black ski mask over his head. Friedrich was enjoying a nice glass of wine while looking at the man.

"Liam, welcome home," Friedrich made this statement while handing a member the almost empty glass of rosé wine.

"Are you ready?" Friedrich asked Liam, just in case he was not mentally prepared.

Liam replied with a simple nod.

Friedrich walked towards the man to unveil his identity. I was not present, but I could only imagine how difficult it must have been for Liam to see that his uncle had betrayed the Society.

"Is he one of yours?" Friedrich asked Liam, who was in complete shock.

"Yeah. He is one of mine," Liam answered in great

pain.

"What would you like us to do with him?" a merciful Friedrich asked Liam.

"Whatever you do with him, it is not my concern."

Friedrich looked at Liam, quite surprised.

"I believe he should be taken to trial, where the leaders of the society will decide if he lives."

Friedrich ordered the man to take him away.

"Why don't we have a drink and discuss our next moves?" Friedrich suggested Liam with an open mind.

"Yes, that would be great!" Liam replied while walking away from the scene.

***

It had all been set up by the leader of Poland for me to find out who the remaining spy was. The member who had betrayed us had been kicked out of the society. The leader of Poland had asked not to speak about him or anything that concerned the society, to avoid further issues. It was around seven o'clock at night, and the leader had invited everyone for dinner. I wasn't planning on attending because a bigger task awaited me. I proceeded to the distinct staff area, where all the personnel were situated. All the employees were diligently working; therefore, it was not a matter of concern to attempt to discover the identity of the remaining spy.

With deliberate caution, I entered the first door lead-

297

ing into the staff area. I dedicated approximately thirty minutes to conducting a comprehensive search of the premises, which included inspecting the bathroom, evaluating the arrangement of furniture, assessing decorative elements, and even examining the air vents. I meticulously checked every possible location for potential evidence or clues.

Unfortunately, the initial three rooms yielded no pertinent information. I proceeded to execute a swift assessment of the remaining rooms but once again found myself at an impasse, unable to uncover any leads that might illuminate the situation. The urgency of my task weighed heavily on me; I was acutely aware of the risks to the Society should I fail to locate the individual in a timely manner.

After taking a moment to gather my thoughts and compose myself, I resumed the search, clinging to the hope that I might soon uncover vital information. However, as time continued to elapse without any significant findings, my frustration mounted, rendering the situation increasingly perplexing. The notion that a single employee could be orchestrating this act of espionage felt implausible, and the inability to find anything of value was disheartening. Just as I prepared to intensify my search, I detected the faint sound of footsteps approaching the vicinity. Instinctively, I moved toward the door and positioned myself to observe through the peephole, eager to ascertain the source of the sound.

It was a woman working as a servant of the house who appeared familiar. I chose not to follow the woman because if she were a spy, she would be aware that I was following her. From the angle I was at, I couldn't see what room she was in. However, she was not too cautious while entering the room, which was quite a relief, since I knew the exact room that she entered. With great caution, I exited the room, heading directly towards the room she had just abandoned. I opened all the bags and drawers and checked the closet to see if I could find something suspicious. Unfortunately, there was nothing to be found.

Even though I had failed to find any hints that would help me find who the remaining spy was. I was lucky to have found a woman entering one of the rooms in a very discreet and stealthy manner. It was unclear to me if the woman was the spy or not; either way, the following thing I was about to do was going to help me figure out who that spy was.

I was never informed, by the leader or members of the Polish society, that the place was being carefully watched by cameras around the house. Something that was not surprising, since it was not difficult to conclude that all the societies act with caution in case an unexpected situation were to occur.

This tactic that the Polish members used was something that I considered to be very intriguing. Members from other societies could easily notice. However, in this particular case, what they had done was very well thought of.

The Polish Society had placed miniature-sized cameras all around the house. The strange thing is that they were not hidden; they were in plain sight, where everybody could see. This explained why they had diverse forms of decorations around the house.

Automatically, I went to my room. Where there was pure peace, enough for me to focus on what I needed to do. I did not waste time using one of the laptops that Malek had provided for me to destroy all the crucial society information from the other laptop at the penthouse, where I was staying. The clock was ticking, and I had no time to waste. Immediately, I accessed the cameras from around the house. From there, I took my time following the women's every move. There was an issue, however, which was that she would not do anything that would make you think that she was a spy. This was concerning because it was unclear to me if she knew that I was watching her.

Everything changed, suddenly, when the image became a bit distorted. It was not something to worry about. That was until I tried all the possible options to fix my screen, but unfortunately, I was unable to. It was at that very moment that I knew the woman was definitely the person that I was looking for.

There was no doubt that I was able to defeat the women in combat. However, I had to be cautious because it was highly likely that she would be able to outsmart me. The lady did not follow a routine, but I do remember the areas where she frequently walked by.

Shortly after, I exited the room and headed straight to the kitchen, where I knew she was most likely not going to see me. Until now, there were no red flags. I observed with keen interest her every move as she entered the kitchen area. However, all she was doing was her job, quickly and effectively.

The employees were busy preparing desserts, the dinner was about to end, and I had been unsuccessful in trying to find anything that could help me find the remaining spy. Having little to no more places to search, I headed to my room, thinking there could be a slight chance that the spy could be a member. Everything changed when the woman put me in a chokehold from behind. Fortunately enough for me, her grip was not too tight, giving me the chance to flip her over and free myself from the chokehold. She quickly jumped back up. At an incredibly high speed, she pulled out a small kitchen knife from her left pocket and would not hold back from viciously attacking me. She was unable to hit me; it was only a matter of time before I disarmed her and knocked her down.

The woman was on the ground, almost paralyzed by the pain I had inflicted on her. A slow clap of hands made me turn around in curiosity. I was somewhat delighted to see that Malek was the person acknowledging what I had done.

"I guess we found whom we're looking for," Malek made this statement while slowly walking in my direction.

The woman was on the ground, making eye contact with me, and it was odd because I had seen that look before. Malek noticed that we were indeed making strange eye contact with one another. He took the wig off her. At the time, I could not believe the woman's identity.

"So, you two know each other?" Malek asked while I stood still with a blank look, not knowing how to reply.

CHAPTER 11

NEW ALLIANCE

Liam was, upon deeper acquaintance, a remarkably affable individual; however, he was also discerning when it came to placing his trust in others. I found it challenging to navigate the dynamic between Friedrich and Liam, particularly after Liam revealed that the individual orchestrating the operation was his uncle. At the bar, Friedrich offered Liam a drink, having instructed the bartender to step away for a more private conversation. Rather than inquiring about Liam's preferences, Friedrich opted for one of their finest wines, meticulously imported from France. The anguish on Liam's face was palpable, and Friedrich recognized that such a moment could weigh heavily on anyone. He advised Liam to move forward, as dwelling on this revelation could impair his judgment and influence his subsequent decisions. While Liam had always exhibited remarkable resilience, this situation marked a rare instance of vulnerability for him. Nevertheless, he ultimately persevered, as he had in every previous challenge. The two men then engaged in a candid discussion about their respective pursuits and values. Friedrich articulated that he held loyalty in high regard, to which Liam concurred, emphasizing that loyalty and passion were integral to true happiness. After what began as a casual conversation, the dialogue transitioned to matters of business, with both men briefly outlining their plans for the Canadian Society. Having moved past his moment of pain, Liam was now resolute in his commitment to safeguarding the one thing he cherished most: the beautiful freedom that his country afforded its citizens.

Liam and Friedrich capped off their long night by making the final decision on what they would do with Liam's uncle. The man responsible for the death of the Austrian leader and the injuries caused to Liam by one of the members. After a few drinks, they decided to send Liam's uncle to trial, where he would most likely be embarrassed in front of all the world leaders of the Society. Friedrich offered Liam to stay at the château, where he would be away from danger. Liam kindly accepted, and their night ended shortly after.

✳✳✳

The Polish leader could not have been prouder of me. Even though I was satisfied with my work, it pained me to find out that the woman I had defeated was someone I had made somewhat of a connection with.

Once the situation had stabilized and tensions had eased, all Polish members, myself included, convened in the conference room. Jelena was bound to a chair in a manner reminiscent of how I presumed Liam's uncle had been restrained. The men in the room exhibited little outward emotion, but it was clear that there was a collective sense of relief at having apprehended the second and final individual involved in espionage against us. Although I was not intimately acquainted with the operations of this particular society, it was evident that secrecy was our most significant asset. The Polish leader had yet to make his entrance, and as members engaged in quiet conversations, I found it increasingly difficult to disregard the fact that Jelena was tied up, likely facing dire consequences. Before long, the leader of the Polish Society entered the room, and it was evident to anyone with a modicum of discernment that he commanded significant respect. He took his place at the head of the table, signaling the commencement of the meeting.

"Malek, please," the all-powerful leader of Poland ordered Malek to remove the black duct tape from Jelena's mouth. She was not shy to spit in Malek's shoes. I turned towards the leader of Poland to see his reaction, but he did not have one at all.

"Tell us who you are, sweetheart," the leader asked Jelena. Who would proceed to spit on the floor.

"I don't think there is anything sweet about her," one of the members said, causing the whole room to burst out laughing. Jelena would not dare to look any of us in the eye and did not bother to answer the leader.

"Jan, escort her out of the room."

Jan, a member of the Polish Society, got up from his chair to escort her out of the room.

"Gentlemen, what should we do with this woman?"

"Treat her as an asset of trade, perhaps, although I believe she has little to no value," one of the Polish members said.

"Charles, where do you know this woman from?" the Polish leader asked me.

"I randomly met her outside of work," I replied, not wanting to give too much information away.

"Since she is not an asset of trade, the most logical solution is to kill her. However, society rules forbid members from killing women."

"What do you want us to do then, sir?"

"We will remain patient for now."

***

It was early in the morning in the small town in Switzerland where Liam was. It had been a great night. The Austrian Society had treated Liam the same way that the Polish Society had treated me, even though we were not members. Liam found himself in a large room with a nice window and enviable views towards the front of the house. The place was safe because it was guarded by members of the Austrian Society 24 hours a day. Liam felt it was not necessary; it would have been difficult to even locate the place. It was not usual for Liam to take a shower early in the morning. However, he felt he needed to take a shower to calm himself down. The bathroom had an old Victorian design, which was quite neat because it made a perfect contrast with the rest of the house. Liam liked his showers cold because they helped his body recover. After taking a long shower, Liam exited the restroom with a white robe he found in one of the cabinets. Liam went back to his room to get dressed. It took him a little while to do so because he had woken up and not meditated. Having time for himself was something Liam valued a lot. For Liam, the only way to train his mind was through meditation. He had always stated that the mind does not rest until you let it do so. Liam sat with his legs crossed on the enormous bed he had slept in. It took him about fifteen minutes to end his session.

Liam made his way to the closet, where the Society had provided him with a fresh change of clothes, consisting of black pants and a burgundy shirt, along with a beautifully polished leather belt that perfectly matched his shoes. Once dressed, he exited the room and traversed the expansive halls of the second floor of the house.

Although this residence was arguably larger than the one I occupied, it exuded a sense of emptiness. The Austrian Society was known for its reluctance to hire unfamiliar individuals, opting instead to work exclusively with those they had collaborated with in the past.

Descending the broad yet steep staircase to the first floor, Liam was met with a suffocating silence that pervaded the house. The dining table was partially set, yet only two members occupied the seats. Liam chose a random chair, remaining silent as the members engaged in their respective activities—one reading a newspaper while the other scribbled notes. It was peculiar that they appeared indifferent to Liam's presence, as he was not a member of the Society. A staff member discreetly filled the glass in front of Liam with water.

As time passed, Liam found himself lost in thought, staring vacantly into space. Gradually, the table began to fill with additional members. Although we lacked detailed insights into the Austrian Society's protocol for selecting a leader, it appeared that Friedrich was poised to assume that role for the next few days. Suddenly, Liam felt a tap on his right shoulder, and without needing to turn around, he instinctively knew it was Friedrich. All members at the table ceased their activities to acknowledge Friedrich's arrival.

"Good morning, gentlemen."

Almost all the members replied to Friedrich.

"For those who do not know, this is Liam; he and I will be confessing in the Grand Society court." Friedrich did not have to speak much, since the members knew the person they were going to trial was the person who had killed their leader.

The members around the house did not say a word; they only listened to what Friedrich had to say.

"While I am away, Klaus will be in charge."

Klaus happened to be the man who was writing when Liam found a seat at the table.

"Are there any questions?" Friedrich asked all the members sitting at the table, although no one replied.

***

Even though I did not have a serious relationship with Jelena, it pained me to know that she had been spying on us. I was confused at that moment; I did not understand who she was working for. But there was one clear rule in the Society: we did not allow any women. For some odd reason, everything clicked. Jelena had been spying on me all this time; luckily, I had suspected that something was wrong. Either way, what she said about her family seemed genuine, although I could not confirm it. All the thoughts swarmed my head.

I found myself seated alone on a stone bench at the rear of the house. The exterior of this residence was so exquisite that it helped me relax and momentarily escape the complexities surrounding me. After finishing my last sip of water, I strolled along the pathways, enjoying the vibrant green grass that filled the air with a refreshing scent. Upon re-entering the house, I discovered I was alone. With little else to occupy my time, I decided to explore the premises at my leisure. I wandered into a room adorned with numerous historical paintings, as the society cherished artifacts that served as reminders of our past. We believed it was essential to honor those who inspired creativity in others. I took a moment to admire a painting by an artist whose name proved to be quite challenging to pronounce.

"Beautiful, isn't it?" Malek made the statement while also enjoying the painting.

"Its simplicity is what makes it beautiful."

"Works of art such as these are never simple. Just like life, there is meaning in everything around us," Malek said, clearly interpreting art differently.

"She does not wish to speak with us."

"Isn't it obvious?" I replied to Malek, who remained by my side.

"I believe you should give it a try," Malek asked with a gentle voice tone. It took me a long time to reply because I was not sure if I had the strength to do it.

"I guess I can try."

"Follow me."

Malek led me to the room where Jelena was. It was still hard for me to enter the room. Malek noticed my hesitant attitude towards speaking to her.

"It will be fine; for the meantime we have paralyzed her body," Malek told me, assuring me she wouldn't be able to harm me. The reason I was so uncomfortable was because of the slight affection I had for Jelena.

Even though it was difficult, I filled myself up with courage and entered the room. Jelena was awake and conscious. However, she was unable to move her body. I stood by the door and stared at her for a few minutes.

"Judging from your appearance, I never would have thought that you were such a great fighter."

"Then you have much to learn," Jelena replied.

"Have you come to kill me?" Jelena asked, without a pinch of fear.

"Why did you get into all of this mess?" Charles asked, disregarding her question.

"The same reason you joined the Society, Charles, we want to protect our people."

"You wanted to protect your people?" I said, not knowing what she meant by the statement.

"Many people have died at the hands of your society."

"The fact that there are some corrupt people in my society does not mean we should all be punished."

"People like you are too powerful, Charles.

The society you belong to has advantages that any government organization can only dream of."

"My intuition tells me that someone from within the Society has hurt you. Revenge does not justify any crime. It makes you equal to the person who instilled grief in your soul."

Jelena looked at me intensely, most likely acknowledging that what I had said was, in fact, true.

"Your fate lies with you, Jelena. My people will not hesitate to kill you if you do not cooperate with us," I said, before exiting the room.

Both Malek and the leader of Poland were waiting for me just outside the room.

"Has the lady eased her opinion on us?" the leader of Poland asked.

"Not sure, but I believe she is taking my words into consideration," I replied.

We then walked to the living room, where all the Polish members were glued to the TV, watching an important soccer match. I sat down on a chair by myself, hoping that I could unwind and enjoy the game just like the rest of the members. Malek went on to give me a glass of white wine before sitting next to me. I had learned that nothing in life was certain, but in the end, with good spirit and a will for freedom, justice, and peace. All the chaos, we fought daily, would come to an END.